D0382083

Poison Ivy and Eyebrow Wigs

OTHER NOVELS BY BONNIE PRYOR

Horses in the Garage
Jumping Jenny
The Twenty-Four-Hour Lipstick Mystery
The Plum Tree War
Seth of the Lion People
Vinegar Pancakes and Vanishing Cream
Rats, Spiders, and Love

Poison Ivy

AND

Eyebrow Wigs

Bonnie Pryor

ILLUSTRATED BY GAIL OWENS

Morrow Junior Books · New York

The poetry quoted on pages 79–80 is from Robert Burns's
"A Red, Red Rose," written in 1847,
and on page 135, "The Purple Cow,"
written by Gelett Burgess in 1895.

Library of Congress Cataloging-in-Publication Data
Pryor, Bonnie.
Poison Ivy and eyebrow wigs / Bonnie Pryor ; illustrated by Gail Owens.
p.   cm.
Summary: Nine-year-old Martin has a busy year in the fourth grade as he tries
to find his own identity both at school and among his large and busy family.
ISBN 0-688-11200-5
[1. Identity–Fiction.   2. Family life–Fiction.   3. Schools–Fiction.]
I. Owens, Gail, ill.   II. Title.
PZ7.P94965Pm   1993
[Fic]–dc20   92-38881   CIP   AC

TO DIRK

Contents

Poison Ivy and Eyebrow Wigs

1

Ice-Cream Disaster

BY THE END of August I was so bored that I actually wanted to go back to school. The first part of summer had been fun. We went camping and Dad got sprayed by a skunk. I'd made friends with our new neighbor, Mr. DeWitt, and he had helped me raise a pumpkin that won first prize at the county fair. Now the garden was limp and old, and I was bored with eating tomatoes and green beans. My best friend, Jamie Jamison, had spent most of the summer at camp. Then he'd been sick with the flu. He was better now, but he always seemed to be busy when I called.

The rest of my family kept scurrying about with all their important things to do. Mom's the mayor of New Albany, where we live. That probably sounds pretty exciting. But she spent half her summer talking to the garbage collectors. They said they wouldn't pick up the garbage unless they got better pay. If anyone had asked me, I would have said they deserved to be paid more. Have you ever smelled inside a garbage can? As usual, no one asked my opinion.

Dad is the most popular doctor in New Albany. He says summer is the worst season for accidents. He's busy day and night fixing broken bones and taking care of bee stings and sunburns. My brother Tim is into sports. He's always off playing baseball or going to swim meets and winning new trophies for his shelves. Then there's Caroline. She's ten, one year older than I am. But she's two grades ahead of me because she's so smart. You wouldn't believe it if you saw the way she acts. In between special classes for gifted children, she spends half her time giggling with her girlfriends and the other half looking for things to tattle about.

My name is Martin Elwood Snodgrass. In addition to having a rotten name, I don't do anything special at all. That's why I spent so much time this summer with Mrs. Albright, our housekeeper, and Robbie, my two-year-old brother, who gives slurpy kisses and wets his pants every ten minutes. I used to look for ways to be famous like the rest of my family. I don't do that anymore, but it still bothers me sometimes. That's why I'd be glad to go back to school. At least there I'd be around regular, everyday sort of people like me.

"I want to get a picture of the family before school starts," Mom announced one evening as we were about to sit down for dinner. "I made an appointment with a photographer for this coming Saturday."

Tim groaned. "Do we have to dress up?"

Mom nodded. Then she turned to me. "Look at your pants, Martin."

I looked down, expecting to see a zipper open or a great big rip. But everything seemed in place. They weren't even very dirty, except for a sticky spot in my pocket where a candy bar had melted.

"What's wrong with them?" I asked.

Caroline snickered and pointed at my bare ankles. "Nothing, if you're expecting a flood."

"It seems that you've been growing this summer," Dad said.

"Maybe now you can play some sports," Tim remarked. "How about basketball?"

"I don't like sports," I explained for the hundredth time.

Tim stared at me as if I were some alien species and shoveled a mountain of potatoes onto his plate. I sighed. Most of the popular kids at school were really good at sports. Maybe I should start pretending that I liked them. Jamie and I had vowed that fourth grade was going to be our best year ever.

"Tomorrow we'd better go shopping for some new outfits," Mom said. "You need some school supplies, too."

"You'd better take him to the beauty parlor." Caroline sneered. "He could get those bushy eyebrows curled."

"That's enough," Dad scolded. "Martin's eyebrows are fine."

Caroline hadn't grown much over the summer, so she didn't need very many new things. I knew she was mad that I was going to get a bunch of clothes. That was why she'd made the remark about my eyebrows. Even so, I worried about it all through dinner.

As soon as we finished eating, I ran to the bathroom mirror to see if my eyebrows were really bushy. They were pretty thick. It was funny I'd never noticed that before. I looked at them for a long time.

I was going to talk to Mom about my eyebrows the next day, but just before we were ready to go shopping, the phone rang.

"That was my aide," she explained when she got off the phone. "The citizens' group against the new highway wants a meeting this afternoon."

This meant that Mrs. Albright would end up taking

me to the mall. I didn't mind. Mrs. Albright is really a super person. She's sort of like an extra grandma, except that she bakes better cookies than either of my real grandmothers.

Since Caroline and Tim were both visiting friends, Robbie had to come with us. We parked at the mall and walked to the biggest department store. Mrs. Albright buckled Robbie into a shopping cart. He liked the little fold-down seat. I pushed the cart up and down aisles to keep him busy while Mrs. Albright looked at sweaters and pants. Robbie hunched over the handle like some crazed motorcycle rider roaring into town.

"Rooom, rooom," he growled at everyone we passed.

"Isn't he cute?" a lady cooed to her husband.

Robbie squinted at her and made another roooming sound. I could see he didn't appreciate being called cute.

"Truck," he declared loudly.

The lady reached over and patted Robbie's head. Robbie's hair is bright red. "Oh, what pretty hair," she said. "Too bad he isn't a girl."

I saw Robbie's mouth open and pushed the cart away just in time. That's Robbie's latest trick. When he gets mad, he bites.

"We have to go now," I said as I hurried him back down the aisle to where Mrs. Albright was looking at some shirts for me.

When we were out of hearing range, I stopped the cart. "People don't bite," I said sternly.

Robbie looked at me out of the corners of his eyes. "Dogs bite," he said. Ever since Robbie could talk, he has pretended to be a dog.

"You are not a dog," I answered, continuing down the rows of suitcases and purses.

"Woof," Robbie said slyly, just as we caught up with Mrs. Albright.

Finally we were done shopping. Except for trying to bite the lady, Robbie was so good that Mrs. Albright decided to stop at a little ice-cream shop in the mall. I ordered a banana split. Mrs. Albright ordered a milk shake for herself and a small dish of ice cream for Robbie. I guess by the time we got to the restaurant, Robbie had been good for as long as he could stand it. First he threw a fit because the waitress brought a high chair.

"No baby chair," he screamed.

Mrs. Albright tried to reason with him. "It's not a baby chair. It's just to make you higher." She picked him up and tried to put him in the chair. But Robbie stiffened his whole body so she couldn't do it.

Everyone in the restaurant was staring at us. "I'll help you bend him," I offered. I tried to fold up his legs so he would sit down. You'd be surprised how strong a two-year-old can be. He just kept himself as stiff as a board, all the time hollering at the top of his lungs.

Mrs. Albright gave up and let him sit in the booth beside her. His eyes came only to the top of the table, but Robbie didn't care. He stood up on the seat and gave Mrs. Albright a big kiss. Robbie's kisses are always wet, so I was glad he was kissing her and not me.

"You little scamp," Mrs. Albright said, shaking her head. I tried to pretend I didn't know Robbie. I probably didn't fool anyone, because we both have the same red hair. Everyone in our family has red hair except Mom. Hers is brown, and she says when it gets gray, she's going to color it red so she looks like the rest of us.

Everyone in the ice-cream shop went back to eating and talking, and I thought for a minute it was going to be all right after all.

Then the waitress brought our ice cream. Robbie had to stand up again to reach his. My banana split was heaped with whipped cream and cherries and nuts. It looked delicious. I saw Robbie eyeing first my dish and then his own. Before anyone could stop him, he reached across the table and dug his spoon into my ice cream.

"Robbie eat 'nana," he shouted. He jerked his spoon up so fast that it caught one whole scoop of ice cream. It was the scoop with the strawberry sauce. It flipped out of the spoon and flew through the air, landing on the top of the booth seat behind Mrs. Albright and Robbie. Strawberry syrup splattered all over Mrs. Albright, and the lady in the booth behind her had little chunks of strawberries in her hair. With a strange squeaking noise, the lady started to jump up, but the scoop of ice cream slipped over the edge of the seat and right down her back.

Mrs. Albright and I were both too horrified to move. We watched as the woman jumped up and did this weird little dance until the ice cream slid down and landed with a plop on the floor.

2

Eyebrow Wigs

ACTUALLY, THE LADY was pretty nice about the whole thing. After Mrs. Albright helped her clean up, apologizing all the while, she actually laughed. "That's the first time I've ever been hit with a flying banana split," she said.

Robbie started crying because he thought the lady had taken his ice cream. "Let's get out of here," Mrs. Albright whispered. She had kind of a desperate gleam in her eyes as she tucked Robbie, still screaming, under her arm and paid the waitress. Out in the parking lot she buckled Robbie into his car seat. He was asleep almost before we pulled out of the parking lot. "Poor little thing," she said. "He was just plain worn out."

I couldn't believe my ears. Poor little thing? What about me? Not only was I humiliated in public, but I'd only had two bites of my banana split.

I was still mad when we got home, although I felt a little better when I looked at all my new school supplies. I thought about school. Last year, I'd been afraid people would think I was a nerd if I admitted I liked math. But this year I was going to try to win first place in the math competition that was held each year. I packed the notebooks and extra paper we'd bought at the mall in my new book bag and went downstairs to sharpen my pencils. Robbie was sitting on the kitchen floor playing quietly with his little cars. He had slept all the way home and was rested and smiling again.

After I sharpened a pencil, I put it on the counter and started on the next one. There were twelve in the box, so it took me quite a while.

"I don't think you need to sharpen them all at once," Mrs. Albright said. She was already mixing up a batch of chocolate chip cookies, and my empty stomach was beginning to growl.

"I like them nice and sharp," I said. "This way I have some extras if I lose one."

Caroline had come home, and she was putting spoonfuls of batter on the cookie sheet. "It's the eraser part

Martin needs the most," she said smugly. "I'll bet you get Mrs. Johnson this year. She's really strict about neat papers. She always gave me stars for neatness."

"My papers are sort of neat," I protested.

"Ha!" Caroline snorted. "You always put an extra hump when you make an *n,* and your *a*'s look like *o*'s."

"She's right," Tim said, walking in the back door in time to catch the end of the conversation. "I had her, too, and she is really strict."

All of a sudden I wasn't so eager to start school. Any teacher who had taught both Tim and Caroline would expect me to be outstanding just like them. There wasn't any chance I wouldn't be recognized, either. Red hair and a last name like Snodgrass are hard to forget.

There was a knock at the back door. "Hi," Jamie Jamison said as he came in. "Want to go bike riding?"

"Boy, am I glad to see you," I answered. I got my bike out of the garage, and we pedaled past Mr. DeWitt's house and turned off on the road past the cornfield. It's mostly flat and there's hardly any traffic, so it's great for bike riding. We raced awhile. Then we slowed down to talk.

"Are you glad school is starting?" Jamie asked.

I nodded. "As long as I don't get Mrs. Johnson. She'll probably expect me to be a great speller like Caroline."

"I'm going to have fun this year," Jamie said. "Have you noticed that I'm not as shy as I used to be?"

I hadn't really, but I nodded.

"Lester and Steve were at camp with me. Can you believe it? The two most popular guys in our grade. We hung around together all month." He paused, and I thought he looked a little embarrassed. "We got to be pretty good friends."

Lester Meyers is really good at baseball and basketball, and Steve Harmon has an indoor swimming pool at his house. Now I understood why Jamie was never home when I called.

"Steve said he was going to invite me to his family's next pool party," Jamie said. "I talked to him about you, and he said he might invite you, too."

Jamie put on his brakes and stood straddling his bike. I stopped beside him. "Don't you get it?" he asked in an excited voice. "If Steve and Lester like you, everyone else does, too. We're going to be friends with all the popular kids in school."

"They're all into sports and stuff like that," I said.

"You're not that bad at basketball," Jamie said. "All you have to do is act cool. And don't say anything dumb, like telling them how you save worms after it rains. Saving worms is definitely uncool."

"Okay." I grinned. I dropped my bike on the roadside and slouched down the road with my thumbs hooked over my jeans pockets. "Is this cool enough?"

"I'm serious," Jamie said.

"Okay, okay," I said. Then I remembered what Caroline had said. "Do you think my eyebrows are too bushy?"

Jamie stared at me so long he almost lost his balance. "Well, they are a little bushy," he finally answered. "But they go well with your freckles," he added quickly.

That was not the answer I was hoping for. In the first place I hate my freckles. And I wasn't sure the popular guys would want someone with weird eyebrows for a friend. There was also the family picture we were having taken on Saturday. I imagined Caroline in about twenty years, showing the picture to her children. "That's Uncle Martin," she'd tell them. "He never had many friends. You can see why when you look at those eyebrows."

"Girls pull out their eyebrows with tweezers," Jamie offered. "I've seen my Aunt Susie do it. But it really looks painful."

"I'll bet I could trim them with scissors," I said. Jamie looked doubtful as we turned our bikes back toward home.

Once we were at the house, we went to my room and I got the new school scissors out of my book bag. "I'll just cut a few hairs off," I said, looking in the bathroom mirror. "Right in the middle where my eyebrows look so fat."

Jamie still looked worried, but I boldly cut where they were the thickest. I turned around for Jamie to see.

13

He tipped his head and squinted. "They're a little crooked. The right one is fatter than the left."

I trimmed a little more and peered at myself in the mirror.

"Now the left one's fatter," I said, cutting some more.

"Oh, my gosh," Jamie exclaimed when I turned around again. "You cut off too much. You've got two little bald spots right in the middle of your eyebrows."

I stepped back from the mirror and took a better look. He was right. There were definitely bald spots. "What am I going to do?" I groaned.

"Maybe you could glue some hair back on until they grow back."

"That's a great idea," I said with relief. "I can use my new school glue."

Jamie looked rather pleased with himself. "There's only one thing, though. School glue washes off."

"Then I just won't wash my eyebrows," I said with a shrug. I brushed up the hairs from the sink into a little pile and went to work. It was harder than it looked, and the glue made my skin feel tight, but in a few minutes the bald spots were covered with hair. I stepped back for Jamie to admire the result.

He frowned. "Worse. The hairs are all going different directions. Your eyebrows look bushier than before."

"I'll just smooth them down," I said. I wet a fingertip and patted the hairs into place.

14

"Hey, that's neat," Jamie declared. "You've got little eyebrow wigs."

"Are you two going to stay in there all day?" Caroline yelled as she pounded on the door.

"We're just leaving," I said, yanking open the door.

"It's about time," Caroline snarled. "What were you doing in there anyway?" She stopped and suddenly broke into giggles. "Is this the new fourth-grade style?" she choked out between laughs.

I ducked back in the bathroom for another look. Now all the carefully glued hairs were stuck in a little glob above one of the bald spots.

"Wait until Mom and Dad see you," Caroline said between gasps. She stopped laughing and gave me a sly look. "Lucky for you I've been reading magazines about makeup and stuff. I could really fix it so they wouldn't notice."

"How?"

Caroline looked smug. "What's it worth to you?"

I sighed. "What do you want?"

"Well, let's see," Caroline said. "I know. You could do all my chores for a month. And if Mom and Dad say anything, you have to tell them that you just wanted to because . . ."—she paused and leaned over and grinned like a vampire about to visit the bloodmobile—"because you love me so much."

"That's too much," I protested.

15

Caroline shrugged. "You can always show Mom and Dad. They might think it's funny." She paused dramatically. "But since we're going to the photographer the day after tomorrow, they might not think it was funny after all."

"I'll do your chores," I said.

"And I used to hate being an only child," Jamie said.

Caroline took Mom's eyebrow pencil out of the medicine cabinet and smiled sweetly. "Martin's glad he's not. If he were, he wouldn't have anyone to rescue him when he did something stupid."

3

The Snodgrass Family Picture

CAROLINE DID A GREAT JOB. Looking at myself in the mirror a few minutes later, I almost thought doing chores for a month was a fair price. First she had lightly stroked the pencil across the bare spots. "Hold still," she ordered when I tried to look in the mirror. Then she glued just a few hairs, to blend in. "There," she said at last, giving me a critical look. "Perfect."

I leaned over to the mirror and stared. Even up close you could hardly tell. My eyebrows even looked a little thinner. "Thanks," I said.

Caroline smiled wickedly. "You don't need to thank me now. You'll be doing it all month."

We went downstairs for the big test. Mrs. Albright is pretty sharp. If she didn't notice my eyebrows, no one would.

Mrs. Albright was just finishing the dishes from the cookie baking. A plate of warm, gooey cookies was on the counter. Jamie took two to eat on his way home. "So far so good," he whispered as he went out the door. Mrs. Albright had looked directly at me twice without seeing anything different.

The next night Mom made us all take a bath. "I made the appointment for ten o'clock tomorrow morning," she said. "That way you should still be clean."

"I have swimming-team practice at eight in the morning," Tim reminded her.

Mom frowned. "I forgot about that, but it will be all right. You can come home at nine and get dressed. By the time we get to the photographer, your hair should be dry."

"Since I'm swimming in the morning, I really don't need a bath tonight," Tim offered.

"I'm sure the people at the YMCA would appreciate your not using the pool as a bathtub," Dad said.

"The people at the YMCA would probably appreciate it if Tim got new tennis shoes." Caroline sniffed and held her nose.

"They're my lucky sneakers," Tim said. "They're the ones I wore when I pitched the no-hitter against Snider's Plumbing."

"Tomorrow you are to wear your good shoes," Dad said. He was probably thinking about being stuck in the car with Tim's sneakers.

Mom sank down in a chair. "Trying to get this family all together for a portrait is harder than scheduling a meeting at City Hall."

Dad bent over and kissed the top of her head. "Relax. I rescheduled all my appointments tomorrow morning, and the kids will be clean and fresh. What could go wrong?"

I agreed with Dad—Mom worried too much. In the bathtub I carefully avoided washing my eyebrows. And for a while the next morning, it looked as if Dad and I were right. At nine o'clock everyone except Tim was lined up on the couch while Mom held inspection. Mom had put a diaper on Robbie so we didn't have to worry about accidents. He looked really cute in his new shirt and bow tie.

Caroline was tugging at her first pair of panty hose.

"They make you look very grown-up," Dad said.

"Do you really think so?" Caroline sounded pleased. She turned to me. "If you didn't know me, how old would you say I looked?"

I started to say ten, but I remembered how she'd

helped fix my eyebrows. "Twelve," I answered, "or maybe even thirteen."

"You look pretty good, too," she said, for once looking at me as if I were something better than an insect.

"This tie is choking me," I said.

Mom started to loosen it. Then came the first crisis. "I can't go," Tim practically shouted as he burst into the house. "Look at my face."

"What's wrong with it?" Dad said, sounding puzzled. "It's the same face you've always had."

"Look at this," Tim said, practically stabbing himself in the nose with his finger.

"It's a zit!" Caroline cried gleefully. "Tim has a pimple right on the end of his nose."

"That's it," Tim roared. "Now I'm really not going."

"I don't care if you have fifty zits. You are going," Mom said sternly. "It hardly shows. We can put a little dab of makeup on it. Anyway, photographs can be touched up so such a tiny pimple doesn't show."

Suddenly the second crisis occurred. "Where is Robbie? It's too quiet," Dad exclaimed.

We scattered instantly to search. Thirty seconds of quiet from Robbie is a danger signal, and this time was no exception. I was the one who found him. He was sitting on the bathroom floor in front of the full-length mirror, rubbing the school glue I'd left in the bathroom into his hair.

"What are you doing?" I yelled.

Robbie looked at me and grinned. "Robbie pretty," he explained, patting his face and admiring himself in the mirror.

Everyone crowded in the bathroom door and stared at me. We had a rule at our house: Anything that cut, spilled, marked, or hammered had to be kept out of Robbie's reach.

"Don't worry. I'll wash it," I said quickly.

"We'll talk about this later," Dad said to me. To Mom he said, "There's still plenty of time. It will wash right out." I held Robbie on the bathroom counter, and in spite of his noisy protests, Dad rinsed out his hair. He fussed so much that a lot of water splashed on me.

Dad toweled Robbie's hair dry and combed it, while I dried my face with another towel. Mom was in Tim's room dabbing makeup on his nose. "There, you can hardly tell," she said.

Tim looked glum, but he put on his jacket. A few minutes later we piled in the car and drove to the photographer's studio.

"I'm Mr. Ginn," a round-faced man introduced himself. He beamed at Mom. "What a handsome family you have, Mayor Snodgrass."

Mom looked pleased as she sat in a velvet chair and Mr. Ginn fussed about. He turned on some bright lights and peeked into his camera. "Now, Doctor Snodgrass,

you stand behind your wife, and the older children can be grouped like so." He frowned slightly as he showed me where to stand. But he smiled again when he looked at Robbie. "This little fellow can sit on his mama's lap." He patted Robbie's cheek. Then suddenly the photographer jumped back. "He—he bit me," Mr. Ginn sputtered.

It was pretty interesting for a few minutes. Mom was scolding Robbie; Dad was soothing Mr. Ginn. Luckily the skin wasn't broken, so after a few minutes Mr. Ginn managed a chuckle. Tim was peeking at his nose in a mirror on the wall, and Caroline and I stood under the bright lights till everything calmed down. I wiped some beads of sweat from my forehead. Finally Mr. Ginn said, "Let's try again."

He looked into his camera and looked up again. "The little fellow isn't smiling." He made funny faces and waved a stuffed clown, but Robbie just stared.

"Martin, please," Mom pleaded. "You can always make Robbie smile." Then she really looked at me, and her eyes grew wide. "Martin," she said with a gasp. "What is that stuck to your nose?"

4

An Oatmeal
Sort of Morning

MOM AND DAD were pretty understanding when I explained how I'd tried to thin my bushy eyebrows. Mom filled in the spots with eyebrow pencil, and we finally managed to sit still for Mr. Ginn. Dad says he's going to hang a large framed print in the living room. It will remind him not to have another family portrait taken until all his children are at least fifty years old.

By the first day of school you couldn't see the bald spots anymore. But I was still worried about getting Mrs. Johnson for a teacher. I woke up at five o'clock and stared at the ceiling, which was the most boring thing

I could think of to do. I figured if I was bored enough, I would go back to sleep. I was too nervous, though. I tried to imagine being in fourth grade. When I was in first grade, the fourth-graders always seemed so big—and smart. Now that I was one, I didn't feel any different than I did last year. I wondered if that was how you grew up. You kept getting older but not feeling any different. Then one day you looked in the mirror and there you were, all grown up.

I thought about Jamie's wanting us to be friends with the really popular kids in school. I wasn't sure what being popular meant. Last year a lot of kids teased me about my name. When they called me Snotgrass, it hurt my feelings and made me feel shy. My only real friend was Jamie. He was the one kid who didn't tease me about my name. We had a lot of fun together, but he wasn't the sort of friend you could really talk to about important things. Jamie was quiet most of the time, and he always got all *A*'s in class. He would never understand how my stomach hurt whenever I had to stand in front of the class.

Last year we did a project about what kind of jobs we'd like to have when we grew up. Jamie had an answer right away—he was going to work on computers in the space program. I'd never told him how worried I was that I'd never be able to decide. It was easy for Tim. He wanted to be a baseball player. Caroline wanted to write, maybe for a magazine. I was the only one in my family who didn't have some special talent. I didn't even know what all the possibilities were. I mean, what if I decided to be a teacher? What if I went to school and studied and studied, and then the day after I became a teacher, I found out I really should have been an elephant doctor in India? I was pretty sure the cool kids never worried about things like that.

I was so busy thinking that now I wasn't even sleepy. Finally I gave up and went to the bathroom to brush my teeth. To my surprise, someone was already in there. I could hear the shower running. I went back to my room and made my bed. That's one of Mom's rules. We all have to make our own beds. The reason we have to make them before breakfast is that Tim used to take so long to eat that he would run out of time to make his bed before the bus came. I don't think it's fair to have to make my bed when I'm practically fainting with hunger, just because of Tim.

After I finished, I picked up the new shirt and jeans I'd chosen the night before and headed back to the bathroom. I could still hear water running.

Ten minutes later it was still running. Tim's door was open a little, so I figured it was him. I wondered if it was possible to fall asleep standing under a shower of water. Maybe he had fallen down and knocked himself out. Why else would anyone, especially Tim, stay in a shower

26

for twenty minutes? I went back to my room, but I kept thinking about Tim, unconscious in the shower. Maybe he was bleeding, and the water was washing it all down the drain. I raced back to the bathroom and pounded frantically on the door. "Tim! Are you all right?"

I heard the water being turned off, and a second later Tim peered out the door.

"What do you want?" he growled.

"I was getting worried. I thought maybe you were hurt or something," I answered.

"I have to get clean, don't I?" Tim said. "It's different when you're in the seventh grade."

This was the same kid who could win the smelliest sneaker contest any day. I must have looked blank, because he added patiently, "Girls."

"You're getting that clean just for girls?" I choked. Obviously Tim had gone crazy overnight. Caroline is a girl. Marcia Stevens at school is a girl. Nobody in his right mind would take a twenty-minute shower for them.

Tim slammed the door in my face, and I headed back to my room. My new shirt still had a tag tied to the button, so I yanked at it. *Pop!* Off came the button with the tag. It sailed across the room and landed somewhere near the bed. Maybe Mom would sew the button on if I could find it, but it was nowhere in sight. I crawled around searching until I finally gave up in disgust and

27

looked in my closet for another shirt. By the time I was dressed, it was getting late, but Tim was still in the bathroom. I picked up my library book and started reading. It was an exciting book called *The Sign of the Beaver* by Elizabeth George Speare, and I read for about fifteen minutes before I tried the bathroom again.

Tim's door was closed, so I figured he had gone to his room to get dressed. That's why I was surprised to see the bathroom door closed and hear the sound of water running. This time Caroline answered my knock. "I got here first. You'll just have to wait," she said, opening the door a tiny crack.

"But I've been waiting for forty-five minutes," I protested.

"Tough," Caroline said as she cheerfully shut the door in my face.

By this time I was getting pretty desperate. There was another bathroom in Mom and Dad's room, but I could hear Dad singing in the shower. There was also a bathroom downstairs for Mrs. Albright. Because Mom's schedule was so crazy, Mrs. Albright lived with us during the week and went home only on weekends. Mom and Dad had given strict orders that Mrs. Albright's room and bath were off-limits at all times.

I went back to my room and tried to read again. Finally, just as I couldn't wait another second, I heard the bathroom door open.

At last! I hurried out as Mom went rushing by with Robbie. "Can you wait a minute, Martin?" Mom said at the bathroom door. "I want to change Robbie. He's pretty wet."

I took one whiff and stepped away from the door. "I'll wait."

Back in my room I double-checked all the supplies in my bag. Mom carried Robbie to his room, and once more I hurried to the bathroom, just in time to see the door closing. Caroline again.

That did it. I pounded on the door. "Let me in there right now," I yelled.

As Caroline opened the door, Mom looked out of Robbie's room with a shocked expression on her face. "Martin, I'm ashamed of you for making a fuss like that."

"But I've been waiting for hours," I protested.

"I just got in here to fix my hair," Caroline whined. "No one cares what you look like," she added with an ugly smirk.

"Martin, it's not like you to be so impatient," Mom scolded.

"I've got to go," I yelled. "Why do I always come last in this family? I wish I were an only child."

"Since you are in such a hurry," Caroline said in her best martyr voice. "I'll let you go in first."

"That's sweet of you, honey," Mom said, giving me

another look. Instead of trying to explain, I rushed in and closed the door. Let them wait for a change, I thought. So I took my time, washing my hands and face and combing my hair as slowly as I could. I brushed my teeth extra carefully. I looked at my watch. Exactly three minutes had passed. What did people do in bathrooms for twenty minutes? If you ask me, spending twenty minutes in a bathroom is even less exciting than staring at your ceiling.

I gave up and left. Caroline was leaning against the wall. "It's about time," she said, pushing past me. "I'm probably going to be late now, because of you."

I went down for breakfast, wondering if my whole day was going to be this bad. The only thing that could make the morning any worse was to have to eat oatmeal for breakfast.

Mrs. Albright usually doesn't arrive on Monday morning until after breakfast, but today she was early. "Good morning," she said cheerfully, as she bustled around the kitchen cooking breakfast. "It's a little nippy out, so I thought you should start off with a good breakfast. I made you a nice warm bowl of oatmeal."

5

Freddie

Now that Tim was in junior high school, he left earlier in the morning. Caroline and I still took the bus together to Pleasant Street Elementary. "Make sure you sit far away from me," she ordered as we walked down the driveway to wait. "I don't want you snooping when I talk to my friends."

"Who would want to listen to you and your friends?" I sneered. "All you do is talk about clothes and giggle over nothing."

"Listen, dinosaur breath. In the first place, my friends and I discuss important things," Caroline replied in a haughty voice. "Unlike some immature fourth-graders I could mention. And in the second place, how do you know what we talk about unless you've been spying?"

Before I could think up an answer, our neighbor Mr. DeWitt stepped out on his front porch. His bushy white eyebrows gave him a fierce appearance, but he was really an old softy. "Going to be kind of quiet around here today," he called. He picked up his yellow cat, Daffy, before she could run after us. "You two have a good day."

"We will," I called back, just as the bus pulled up. I climbed up the steps and looked around quickly. Caroline's friends had saved her a seat in the back with them. The bus was already crowded. The only place left to sit was right behind the driver, next to a little kid with a missing tooth. This day was getting worse by the minute. With a sigh I sat down.

"Look what I've got," the boy said. Rummaging around in his pocket, he at last pulled out a wrinkled dollar bill. "For my tooth. See?" He proudly pointed to the empty space in his mouth. "The tooth fairy took it last night and gave me a whole dollar."

"That's great," I told him. A notice from school had just come the day before. I pulled the notice out of my book bag and pretended to study it. It said I was in room 201. That was Mrs. Johnson's room but at least it was upstairs, away from all the little kids.

"My name is Freddie," the boy said. "Bet you can't guess how old I am."

"Six?" I guessed.

Grinning broadly, Freddie shook his head.

"Five? Seven?"

"Nope. Guess again."

"I give up," I said.

"I'm only one." Freddie laughed.

"That's impossible," I said. "You can't go to school if you're one."

"I can," Freddie said. "My birthday is on February twenty-ninth, so I've only had one birthday. My mom does give me a cake on February twenty-eighth," he admitted. In the same breath he asked, "What room are you in?"

"I'll be upstairs with the big kids," I answered.

"Oh," Freddie said a little wistfully. "I was hoping you'd be in first grade." He was silent for a minute. "I don't know where I'm supposed to go. I wanted my mom to come, but she couldn't get off from work."

I wanted to ignore him. It's not a good idea to start fourth grade with everyone thinking you play with first-graders. But when I looked at him, I remembered that when I was little, the first day of school was always scary. Kindergarten was the worst. Dad had opened his office late that morning, and both Mom and Dad had gone with me. Even so, I'd almost thrown up as we walked down the hall to the kindergarten room. Mom went with me the first day of first grade and second grade, too. It would be scary to go by yourself.

"Want me to help you find your room?" I offered reluctantly.

Freddie's face lit up with a grin, and he nodded. For the rest of the trip he chattered about tooth fairies and his dog Cinder, and gave me a day-by-day description of kindergarten last year.

By the time the bus pulled up in front of the old brick school, I was already regretting my offer to walk Freddie to his room. Naturally, the first person to notice us was Willie Smith.

"Hi, Snotgrass," he yelled, loud enough for everyone on the playground to hear. "Going back to kindergarten?"

I groaned. It didn't bother me so much to be called Snotgrass anymore, but Willie Smith was the last person I wanted to run into right now. Willie was the sort of person trouble seemed to follow. If there was something broken, it was probably Willie's fault. Heard a strange noise in the room? Willie was probably there. He laughed when he should have been quiet, and was silent when he should have talked. He was the kind of kid who likes to sit in the very back row, and the teachers always move him to the seat in front of their desks. Willie was older than the other fourth-graders because

he'd been in third grade twice. I think they only let him go to the fourth grade this year because the third-grade teachers couldn't stand him another year. I could see that he'd grown even more over the summer. The girls all thought that Willie was good-looking with his curly black hair and deep blue eyes. But I noticed that he needed a haircut, and his wrists stuck out of the frayed cuffs of his shirt.

Freddie drew himself up to his full height of three and a half feet. "I am not in kindergarten," he declared loudly. "I'm in the first grade."

Willie laughed. "You'd better eat a lot of spinach. That will make you grow. Then you can be big and tough like me." He flexed his muscles like a weight lifter.

"Martin's taking me to my room," Freddie said, inching a little closer to me.

"Where's your mom or dad?" Willie asked.

"She had to work," I explained, hoping Willie wouldn't spread it all over school that I was escorting first-graders.

"I'll walk with you," Willie offered.

"That's okay," I said quickly. "I can do it."

Willie shrugged. "Maybe it will make us late. I'm not that anxious to go to my room. I've got Mrs. Johnson," he added.

"So do I," I said.

"Hey, that's great, Snodgrass. We'll be in the same room again."

"Yeah, that's great," I said, almost meaning it. Actually I kind of liked Willie, but I just wasn't sure I wanted to be in the same classroom with him.

6

Love

"DID YOUR MOM take you to school when you were in first grade?" Freddie asked Willie while we walked in the school door.

Willie shrugged. His voice was gruff. "Naw. She split when I was five."

We found Freddie's classroom and delivered him to his teacher. By the time we ran upstairs to room 201, the bell was about to ring. I searched the row of lockers until I saw the one with my name and stuffed my book bag into it. Willie grabbed a seat in the very back of the room, just as I figured he would. I looked around quickly as I headed for the one empty seat. Most of the kids had been in my room last year. Jamie was one seat ahead of me, two rows over, but sitting primly next to him was Marcia Stevens. I sighed. Marcia is a real pain. She's kind of cute because she wears these round glasses that make her look like an owl. But she is the worst tattletale in school.

I tried to remember what Mrs. Albright had packed in my lunch. Maybe I could bribe Marcia into changing seats. Just as I was about to offer her a piece of Mrs. Albright's chocolate cake, an angel walked into the room.

Of course it wasn't really an angel, but she was the most beautiful person I'd ever seen. If you were going to draw an angel, you'd want her to be your model. Her eyes were big and very blue, and her skin was pale and soft-looking. Her blond hair was curly and long, and it fluffed around her face like a halo.

"Good morning, class." Her voice was soft and warm, as I knew it would be. "My name is Miss Lawson. I'm going to be your teacher this year."

There was a minute of stunned silence. Marcia raised her hand, her face scrunched up with suspicion. "Where is Mrs. Johnson? I'm supposed to have Mrs. Johnson for a teacher this year."

"Mrs. Johnson has made the decision to take some time off because she is having a baby. I am going to take her class this year. I hope you aren't too disappointed."

Disappointed? Would anyone be disappointed to have an angel for a teacher?

Although Miss Lawson was still talking, my heart was pounding too hard to hear. I looked around to see if anyone else felt the same way. Jamie was staring at Miss Lawson with his mouth hanging open. Steve, Lester, and Kyle were poking one another and winking. Even Willie was sitting up straight, listening to her every word. Marcia was still frowning, but then Marcia frowns at everything.

Everyone had to stand up and say his or her name while Miss Lawson made a seating chart. When that was done, she stood in front of the class.

"I'll tell you a little bit about myself. I moved to town a few weeks ago, so I don't know very many people here. This is my first year teaching. I've wanted to be a teacher since I was about your age, and I'm really happy that at last my dream has come true. I like animals, especially dogs and cats. This summer I went on a whale-watching trip, and when we study whales later this year, I'll show you the pictures I took. Oh yes, and my favorite food is pizza. I think we are going to have a wonderful year together."

Miss Lawson paused and smiled at all of us. "Now I've told you about myself. While I'm passing out the reading books, I would like you all to write something about yourselves. Just pretend we are new friends meeting for the first time, and tell me the things I should know."

Marcia waved her hand in the air. "How long does it have to be?"

Miss Lawson paused for a minute. "Let's say one page . . . in regular-sized writing."

Steve raised his hand. "Does spelling count?"

Miss Lawson shook her head. "Not this time."

Marcia's hand went up again. "I had the starring role in the community Youth Theater production of *Annie* last year. Would you like to know about that?"

"Whatever you think is important," Miss Lawson said patiently.

"I think it's very important. My mother thinks I should be an actress when I grow up. I don't know if I can tell you all about it in one page. Can it be longer?"

Miss Lawson nodded. "But not too much more. I just want to know a few important things about you. You can get started now while I pass out some books."

I took out a piece of paper and one of my sharp pencils. Here was my chance to tell Miss Lawson something really great about myself. I stared at the paper. What was important about me?

Everyone else was busy writing. Willie was hunched over his desk, frowning. Suddenly he blurted out, "Can we make some stuff up?"

All the kids laughed, but Miss Lawson's answer was

a little sharp. "Of course not. I asked you to tell me about yourself."

"I can make music with my armpits," Willie said. He demonstrated with several loud noises.

"Gross," said Marcia. Some of the other girls giggled, and most of the boys tried to make the same noise.

Miss Lawson made an effort to regain order. "I'm sure you can think of something a little more interesting about yourself."

Willie looked as if he were really thinking. Then he burped loudly. "I can do that, too," he said.

The class roared with laughter. "That's enough!" Miss Lawson did not sound like an angel now.

I thought about Willie not having a mother and his clothes always being a little too small. Maybe he didn't like to tell people about himself. But Miss Lawson frowned, and looked down at her seating chart. "Just do the best you can."

Willie bent back over his paper. I glanced at Marcia, who was scribbling furiously. Even with her small, scrunchy writing, she had nearly filled her paper. She evidently had a lot of facts to tell Miss Lawson.

I could have written everything important about her in one sentence: I am a *pain*.

Just then, Marcia looked up. "You'd better get busy," she hissed, covering her paper with her arm so I couldn't see.

"You'd better mind your own business," I accidentally said out loud. Miss Lawson looked up from her desk, but before she could speak, Marcia jumped up. "Miss Lawson, Martin's bothering me. And he hasn't even started writing."

That was when I fell in love. Miss Lawson didn't yell or even frown. Instead, she smiled her angel smile. She glanced at the seating chart. "Sit down, Marcia. I'm sure Martin is just thoughtfully choosing his words."

Suddenly I wanted to tell Miss Lawson everything about me. I knew she was exactly the sort of person who would understand. My pen flew across the paper.

My name is Martin Snodgrass. I will be ten years old on November thirtieth. Most people like me, but this year I would like to be really popular.

Here is what is bad about me.	*Here is what is good about me.*
1. My name.	*1. I'm nice to animals and*
2. My red hair.	*bugs.*
3. I'm not very good at	*2. I like to grow gardens.*
sports.	*3. I'm good at math.*

P.S. I think you are beautiful.

7

Dandruff and Naked Dogs

AFTER WE GOT OFF the bus that afternoon, Caroline went straight into the house, and I stopped next door to visit Mr. DeWitt. It might seem strange that I'm good friends with an old man, but we get along great. Mr. DeWitt and I rescued his yellow cat, Daffy, when she had a broken leg. Mr. DeWitt fixed it, and now she hardly limps. Daffy was sitting on the steps. I picked her up and scratched her ears until she started to purr.

"Quick! Come inside," Mr. DeWitt said when he opened the door. "My son is going to be on television any minute."

Mr. DeWitt's son was a real actor in California. "Is he in a movie?" I asked as I sat down in front of the set.

"There he is!" Mr. DeWitt shouted. His son was on the screen telling a friend how to get rid of dandruff. It was pretty embarrassing. Would you tell the whole world you used to have dandruff? But it didn't seem to bother Mr. DeWitt. He looked terribly pleased when he turned off the television.

"How was your first day in fourth grade?"

"Pretty good," I answered. "I looked in my math book, and we're going to have fractions and decimals this year." I told him about walking Freddie to class, and about how much I'd liked Miss Lawson. "Have you ever been in love?"

Mr. DeWitt looked at me for a minute. "Once or twice," he answered.

"Then you probably know what girls like," I said.

Mr. DeWitt scratched his head thoughtfully. "When I was going with Mrs. DeWitt, I used to write her poems. She liked that. And sometimes I brought her flowers."

I jumped up. "Those are great ideas. Thanks a lot."

I waved good-bye and hurried home. Robbie met me at the door. "Look, Martin. All dry," he said, proudly handing me his underpants. Other than his socks and shoes, he was completely naked.

"That's great," I told him. "But don't you think you should put them on?"

He pointed to himself. "Doggie. No clothes."

"There you are, you little scamp." Mrs. Albright came running up with a bundle of clothes in her arms.

Robbie ducked behind me. "No clothes," he said.

Mrs. Albright made a grab for him, but Robbie darted around me and headed out the door. "No clothes!" he shouted at the top of his lungs.

It happened so fast that I just stood there. Mrs. Albright dashed after him, huffing and puffing and still hanging on to the armful of clothes. Robbie was running as fast as his little legs would go across the front yard.

Even though we live outside town and a huge cornfield borders part of our yard, the road in front of the house is a two-lane highway. Robbie has a small, fenced-in play area in the backyard, and he's not allowed in the front yard. Usually the traffic is pretty fast, but now several cars slowed down to watch the chase. I could see the drivers laughing.

Mr. DeWitt saw Robbie and ran over from his yard to head him off. By now I had come to my senses and circled around the other way. When the three of us had him cornered, Robbie finally stopped running. Still, he wanted the last word. He opened his mouth and howled in loud protest as Mrs. Albright tried to stuff him back in his clothes.

"He thinks he's a dog," I told Mr. DeWitt.

He tried to help. "Look, Robbie. Martin wears clothes."

Robbie kept howling, but he peeked out of the corner of his eyes to see if it was true.

I patted my shirt. "I like clothes," I said.

His howl died down to an indignant roar. "I like your shirt," I said encouragingly.

Robbie sniffed. "Pretty?"

"Very pretty," I assured him.

"Looks like you really have your hands full with that young fellow," Mr. DeWitt remarked.

"Thank you for helping us catch him," Mrs. Albright said.

"That's all right," he answered, smiling. "It gives me a good excuse to talk to you. It's a shame to be right next door to such a pretty lady and hardly ever see her."

Mrs. Albright looked flustered, and her face got red. "I'm usually busy in the house," she said. She took Robbie's hand and started to walk to the house. After a few seconds, she stopped. "I do sit out with Robbie in the morning while he plays. I suppose we could visit a bit then."

Mr. DeWitt nodded. "That would be nice."

"Well, I'd better get Robbie back indoors," she said. Mr. DeWitt looked pleased as he headed to his house.

I went along with Mrs. Albright and Robbie. "Mr. DeWitt is a really nice person," I said. "When he first moved in, we all thought he was a grouch, but he was just lonely."

Mrs. Albright nodded. "He is very nice." Then she knelt down and straightened the buttons on Robbie's shirt, and her face looked thoughtful. "Do your mother and father plan on having any more children?" she asked.

8

Teacher's Pet

THE NEXT MORNING I thought about a poem for Miss Lawson. But I had to give up any ideas I had about writing it during the bus ride.

Once again the only empty seat was next to Freddie. He gave me a gap-toothed grin as I sat down. "I'm glad I have a best friend to sit with on the bus."

"I'm not your best friend," I said crossly, trying not to look at his face.

"Isn't there anyone in your room on the bus?" I asked, twisting in my seat to see. "How about those guys back there?" I pointed to two first-graders in the backseat who were devouring the goodies out of their lunch sacks.

"They don't like me," Freddie answered solemnly. "They said my ears stuck out."

"Your ears look okay to me," I said.

"That's why you're my best friend." Freddie gave me another grin, showing the empty spot where his tooth had been. Then he launched into a story he had dreamed the night before. There was a spaceship, some totally weird creatures, and a hero named Freddie. I had a feeling he was adding details as he went along.

Freddie dashed off to his classroom as soon as the bus pulled up at school. I started thinking about a poem again until I noticed something great. There is a fence around the school grounds, and growing around it were bunches of pretty little blue flowers. Here they were growing wild, but Mr. DeWitt had some in his garden, and he said they were called bachelor's buttons. Although I grabbed several handfuls, bachelor's buttons are small, and the bouquet looked kind of puny. I looked at the flowers, wondering what I could do to make them a little more spectacular. Then I remembered that we had bought some flowers for Mother's Day. When we couldn't afford very many flowers, the florist tied a few carnations with a bow and put them in a box. I didn't have a box but my new notebook came with a few sheets of lined colored paper that were pretty nice. I laid the flowers sideways and wrapped the paper around the stems like a cone. That made it look a little bit better, but it was still small. Then I remembered something else. The florist had added some leaves with them. It was almost time for the bell to ring, so I had to work fast.

I grabbed a few leafy stems growing nearby and stuck them in with the flowers.

Willie Smith gave me a friendly wave from across the playground. "Hey, Snodgrass. What are you doing?" he shouted.

"Nothing," I said, hurrying through the gate just as the bell rang. I tried to hide the flowers as we filed in, but Willie had already seen.

"Are those for Miss Lawson?" he demanded.

I shrugged, trying to ignore him, but he kept following me. "Martin wants to be teacher's pet," he teased loudly as we entered the room.

The room was suddenly quiet, and everyone stared at me. Then Lester and Steve started to laugh. I felt my face get hot, and I glared at Willie. "I do not," I shouted. I started to throw the flowers in the wastebasket by Miss Lawson's desk—too late. Before I could get rid of it, Miss Lawson walked into the room and spied the bouquet.

"Oh my, are these for me?" she asked, taking the bouquet and sniffing them.

"I don't think they smell very good," I told her. "But I thought they were a pretty blue."

"My favorite color," she said. She took a little vase

from the shelf and handed it to me. "Will you go to the fountain and fill this with water?"

Feeling everyone's eyes on me, I went out the door. It was a warm day and my hands felt itchy. I filled the vase and rinsed off my hands in the cool water. When I brought back the vase, Miss Lawson was still holding the flowers while she explained to Marcia and Josh about passing out the new math books that were stacked on the table. She rubbed her nose and scratched the back of her hand. "I wonder if I'm allergic to bachelor's buttons." She chuckled.

Then Miss Lawson looked at the flowers and dropped them on the floor. "Oh no," she moaned.

9

Poison Snodgrass

THE WHOLE CLASS froze in surprise.

"Is there a bug or something?" I asked, jumping up in alarm.

Miss Lawson's nose twitched. She stared at her hands in horror. At the same time I took a good look at the leaves I'd used for decoration. "Poison ivy," we gasped in the same breath.

"It will help to wash our hands," I said. I glanced down at my own hands. Little bumps were coming up all over them.

Miss Lawson nodded. "I think you're right, Martin."

53

She turned to the class. "Everyone remain seated. Marcia, you're in charge."

Marcia walked briskly to the front of the room, ignoring all the groans. "Don't worry. I'll take care of them," she said.

Miss Lawson looked at my hands. "Go to the rest room and wash your hands two or three times with soap. I'll go to the teachers' lounge and do the same thing. Then I'll meet you at the nurse's office."

A loud guffaw came from the back of the room. "Way to go, Snodgrass." It was Willie Smith, naturally. Marcia was cringing away from me, looking as if I were the creature from the black lagoon.

My ears turned purple with embarrassment. How could I have done such a dumb thing? And to Miss Lawson, of all people. I'd gotten poison ivy on my hands earlier in the summer, and Mr. DeWitt told me how to watch out for its three shiny leaves. I stumbled out of the room and raced down the hall to the rest room.

I washed carefully with soap and did it again to make sure I got the poison ivy all off. Washing did seem to help. The itchiness was almost gone. I wondered if Miss Lawson could get it all off her hands before she broke out. I thought of her face as I'd handed her the flowers. She had been so pleased. She had . . . Suddenly a horrible picture came into my mind. Miss Lawson had smelled the flowers. She had put her nose right in them.

I ran down the hall to the teachers' lounge. "Miss Lawson," I screeched.

Mr. Higgenbottom, the principal, met me at the door with a disapproving stare. "What is all the commotion about, Martin?"

"I just wanted to tell Miss Lawson that she should wash her nose."

Mr. Higgenbottom looked puzzled. "Miss Lawson's nose is dirty?"

Miss Lawson came out of the teachers' lounge. "Martin presented me with a lovely bouquet. Unfortunately it had a few sprigs of poison ivy," she said. "But I've washed carefully, including my nose, so maybe we will be lucky," she added with a rueful smile. She turned to me. "Don't feel too bad. I know you were trying to do something nice. And it really was a lovely thing to do."

The nurse gave us some pink stuff to rub on our skin. I followed Miss Lawson back to class. She was being so nice that it made me feel even worse. I almost wished she would yell at me or something.

Marcia had the class organized for a spelling bee when we got back to the room. Everyone was lined up against the wall, except for Willie. He was hanging out the window so far that his feet were almost off the ground.

"Willie!" Miss Lawson called sharply. "Get back in before you fall."

Willie jumped back in so fast, he bumped his head on the window. "My pencil fell out," he explained. "I was trying to see where it went."

Miss Lawson handed Willie a pencil from her desk. "You may use this pencil to write fifty times, 'I will not throw things out the window.' "

The room became very quiet, and everyone sat back down, looking uncomfortable.

Jamie was grinning. I saw him pointing to Lester behind his hand. Lester looked smug.

"I didn't throw it out the window," Willie protested.

"Then who did?" Miss Lawson asked.

Willie shrugged. "It just accidentally fell out."

"Willie said it was hot and opened the window," Marcia offered. "But I didn't see what happened after that. I was giving out the spelling words."

"It doesn't really matter," Miss Lawson said. "Nothing would have happened if Willie had been in line for the spelling bee like everyone else."

Willie took the new pencil and walked to his desk. On the way he passed Lester's desk and kicked his ankle.

"Ow," Lester yelled.

"I think you had better see Mr. Higgenbottom," Miss Lawson said. She hastily scrawled a note and handed it to Willie. "You may take this to him." Willie shrugged and slouched out the door. I gave him a sympathetic look, but Willie grinned as he passed my desk.

Miss Lawson beamed at Marcia. "A spelling bee—what a good idea. You'd be a good teacher."

Marcia looked pleased. Then she glanced at me and frowned. "Do I have to sit by Martin? My mother says I am very allergic to things."

"Things? Are you saying you believe that you are allergic to Martin?" Miss Lawson asked.

Marcia sniffed in my direction. "Martin is covered with poison ivy."

"I don't think you will catch poison ivy just by sitting next to Martin," Miss Lawson said patiently.

"But what if he touches me?"

A ghost of a smile passed over Miss Lawson's face. "Martin, will you give me your word of honor not to touch Marcia?"

That was the easiest promise I ever made. "With pleasure," I said.

10

Doggie Takes a Walk

OF COURSE CAROLINE heard about what happened. She blabbed out the whole story to Mom and Dad that night. "Can you imagine anything so dumb?" she asked.

Dad's mouth twitched at the corners. "In my day we gave the teachers apples or little cups to hold pencils." He inspected my hands. "Looks as though you got off pretty easy."

"Martin could go into business," Tim said. "He could call it 'Martin's Deadly Bouquets.' "

Mom patted my shoulder. "I'm sure Miss Lawson

knows you meant well. Don't worry. Tomorrow it will all be forgotten."

The next morning, however, Miss Lawson was absent. "I'm afraid Miss Lawson has had a rather bad reaction to the poison ivy," Mr. Higgenbottom explained. My heart sank. Miss Lawson had been pretty nice when it happened, but Caroline was right. Giving a teacher a poison ivy bouquet was the dumbest thing anyone could do. Maybe Miss Lawson even hated me by now. Although I kept my eyes glued to Mr. Higgenbottom, I could feel everyone glaring at me as he introduced the substitute, Mrs. Sewall.

At morning recess Marcia and several of her friends walked by me, singing noisily, "Poison ive-ee-e, poison ivee-e." I tried to ignore them, but Jamie looked embarrassed. "I told you not to do anything dumb. Couldn't you just have given Miss Lawson an apple out of your lunch?" he asked.

"I wanted it to be something special. I really like her," I confessed.

Jamie laughed. "She is pretty. But she's old. I'll bet she's at least twenty. Martin's in love with Miss Lawson," he said loudly as Steve and Lester walked by.

I couldn't believe Jamie was acting like that. Then I realized he was trying to show off for Lester and Steve. Surprisingly, Steve grinned at me. "Did you see her face when she realized it was poison ivy? That was the funniest thing I ever saw. I gave her an orange. My mom always puts them in my lunch, but I hate to peel them." Suddenly I knew that Steve thought I'd given Miss Lawson the poison ivy on purpose.

Lester looked around the playground. "Come on. We're wasting time standing here. Let's shoot some baskets." He paused and looked at me. "You do like to play basketball, don't you? I remember last year you—"

I saw Jamie's warning glance and didn't let him finish his sentence. "I like basketball a lot now."

"You probably won't get much chance to shoot baskets," Steve warned. "Lester and I are on the YMCA team. We're pretty good."

Marcia and Elizabeth were playing catch with a big ball close by. As we started over to the basketball hoop, the ball got away from them and rolled toward us. Lester scooped it up and tossed it to Steve.

"Give that back," Marcia fumed. "We were playing with it."

"Oh, I'm sorry," Steve teased. "Here. Take it back." Then instead of tossing it to Marcia, he threw it over his head to me. Luckily, for once I managed to catch it. I wasn't very happy with Jamie, so I threw it high over Marcia's head to Lester. Marcia and Elizabeth ran back and forth, but we managed to keep the ball away from them until the bell rang.

"You made us miss the whole recess," Marcia said, glaring at us. "I hate all of you."

Lester swaggered in the door, laughing. "That was fun."

I laughed, too. It had been fun seeing Marcia so frustrated.

At lunch recess the girls figured out a way to get back at us. If we tried to swing, a group of girls was standing in front of the swings. If we ran races, girls would walk in our path. Marcia had all the girls in the room on her side. Everything we tried to do, the girls would be in the way. When Steve yelled at Amy and Marcia, the playground monitor scolded him.

"We have to stick together and think of a way to get even," Lester said, just as the bell rang.

Steve raised his fist in the air and grinned at me. "This is war." I grinned back. Steve and Lester were acting as if Jamie and I were good friends.

Marcia stuck out her tongue every time she saw me. In spite of feeling bad about Miss Lawson, it was a pretty good day.

But it wasn't so great at home. At home, there was Caroline. "What a dweeb. What a jerk," she said every time she passed me.

Dad's office was in the back of our house. On Wednesday afternoons he stopped seeing patients at three o'clock. He looked up from the medical journal he was reading in the family room. "That's enough," he scolded after she'd said it for the third time.

"Robbie wet pants," my little brother announced.

Mom put a new pair of training pants on him and sat him on the floor so he could play with his cars.

"Don't make Martin feel any worse than he does," Mom told Caroline after she'd called me a name for about the tenth time. "It was an accident. It might have happened to anyone."

"Well, it didn't happen to anyone. It happened to my dumb brother," Caroline told her. "And now every teacher in the school is giving a nature lesson on identifying poison ivy." She gave me a pointed look. "Some of us already knew. I'll bet everyone in the whole school is laughing at you."

"They are not," I protested hotly. "Steve and Lester are the two most popular fourth-graders. And they played with Jamie and me every recess."

"Who are Steve and Lester?" Mom asked.

"A couple of fourth-grade jerks," Caroline answered for me. "They're big sports jocks like Tim."

"Do you like them?" Dad asked, sounding a little surprised.

"They're okay," I said. "Jamie really wants to be friends with them."

"I don't think friends need to like all the same things," Mom said. "But it helps if you share some interests."

"They are all interested in being jerks," Caroline said.

"Don't forget that I know where the poison ivy

grows," I said, giving her the meanest look I could. "How would you like to wake up some morning sleeping in a bed full of it?"

"Ha!" Caroline crowed. "Mr. Higgenbottom had the custodian get rid of it. It's all gone."

"I said that's enough, both of you," Mom said sternly. "I have to attend the city council meeting tonight, and I'd like to enjoy a peaceful dinner before I go."

Mrs. Albright set a heaping platter of fried chicken on the kitchen table. "Dinner's ready," she announced. We all trooped out of the family room.

"Let's wash your hands, Robbie." Mom looked around the kitchen. "Where is Robbie?" she asked.

"He was with us just a minute ago," Caroline said.

Tim chose that moment to arrive home from swimming practice. "Hey," he called, "the front door is wide open, and Robbie's clothes are piled out in the yard!"

We all ran into the front yard. Robbie's shirt, pants, and the training pants Mom had just put on him were lying in a little heap.

"He must have learned how to open the door," Mom cried. Up until now the knob had been too hard for Robbie to turn.

Tim was standing at the edge of the highway, looking up and down the road. "No sign of him here," he called.

"Then don't panic," Dad said. "He can't be far. Maybe he's over at Mr. DeWitt's house."

63

Caroline made a funny noise in her throat. "Wherever he is, he's naked."

I ran over to Mr. DeWitt's house. A quick glance around the yard told me Robbie wasn't there, but I knocked anyway. Mr. DeWitt answered the door and shook his head when I explained. "Did you check the house?" he asked.

This was not the first time Robbie had disappeared. Once I thought he was lost in the cornfield behind our house, and we had even called the police to help us look before I found him in the house asleep. "He's not in the house this time," I said, explaining about the discarded clothes.

"Lucky it's still warm outside." Mr. DeWitt shook his head again. "Let's check my garage."

I followed him to the garage, but it was empty. We searched and called for several minutes, but there was no answer from Robbie. Dad scanned the farmer's field. It had already been cut, and it was easy to see that Robbie had not headed that way.

"Maybe we should call the police," Mom said.

"He's got to be around here somewhere," Dad said. "How far could a two-year-old go in ten minutes?"

"Pretty far, if it's Robbie," Tim started to say, when suddenly we heard the wail of sirens. There was a small housing development down the road from Mr. DeWitt's house. Mom and Dad looked at each other and without a word went running in that direction.

"What if something terrible happened?" Caroline cried.

There was a huge lump in my throat that made it hard to swallow. I realized how much I loved the little guy. "Please," I prayed silently. "Make this okay, and I'll never get mad at him again."

As we all ran toward the development, we could see several parked cars and a small crowd of people. Mom grabbed Dad's hand, her face pale with worry. Dad pushed his way through the crowd. "I'm a doctor," he shouted. "Let me through." The crowd parted enough that I could squeeze in behind Dad. I peeked around several people, almost afraid of what I would see.

It was Robbie, all right. But he wasn't hurt. Someone had wrapped a towel around his waist, and someone else had given him a big sucker. The police officer was kneeling down, writing in his notebook. He grinned when he saw Mom and snapped it closed.

"We found this little fellow taking a stroll down the street. I thought this was one of yours, Mayor." He chuckled. "Hard to disguise that red hair."

Someone in the crowd snapped a picture. Robbie grinned from ear to ear, pleased at all the attention. "Hi, Martin," he said. "Doggie take walk."

11

Robbie Makes the News

"You did okay with Tim and me," Caroline told Mom and Dad the next night. She threw down the evening paper with a sigh. "Why didn't you stop while you were ahead?"

"Now, Caroline," Dad said.

"First Martin, and now Robbie. Everyone in town must be laughing at us."

"Maybe the paper didn't have very much news today," Tim said. "No wars or anything. So they decided to fill in with this." He doubled over with laughter.

I picked up the paper and looked at the article again.

Robbie's picture was on the front page. It showed him wrapped in the towel, licking his sucker and grinning. "Robbie Takes a Stroll" was the caption under the picture.

"I don't find it the least bit funny. Just wait until election time. My opponent will have a ball with this." Mom looked pretty glum.

I read the article under the picture. " 'Mayor Snodgrass's youngest son took a stroll today *au naturel.*' " I looked up. "What does *au naturel* mean?"

"It means he was naked, dummy," Caroline answered.

"People must think I'm an awful mother," Mom moaned.

"Not if they know Robbie. Maybe we should get a leash," I suggested. "Then you could tie him up."

"He's a little boy," Mom scolded. "Not a dog."

"Woof," Robbie said.

"If we had a real dog, maybe Robbie would stop pretending he's one," I suggested hopefully. Over the summer I'd overheard Mom and Dad talking about getting a puppy for my birthday, but that seemed like a long time to wait.

"We know how much you'd like a pet. We thought we'd wait for your birthday and get a puppy then," Mom admitted.

"If you got a dog now, Martin couldn't say it was just

his," Caroline pointed out. "It would belong to the family."

"Real dogs are a lot of work," Dad said.

"We'll all help," I said. "I would feed it and brush it."

Mom and Dad looked thoughtful, so I tried harder. "We could train the dog to bark every time Robbie went out the door."

"A dog could guard the house when we're not home," Caroline added.

"I have a better idea. Dad is putting a lock high up on the door. And one of us will watch Robbie every minute until he gets over this stage," Mom said.

I wanted to talk about getting a dog some more, but just then the phone rang. "Hello, Martin," Miss Lawson said when I answered. "I was wondering how you were."

I was so surprised, I could hardly answer. Miss Lawson was sick enough to miss school, and she was still thinking about me. She *was* an angel. "I'm okay," I said. "I have only a little itchy spot on my arm. Are you all right?"

"I'll be fine in a couple of days," Miss Lawson answered. "The doctor gave me some pills, and they're helping a lot. I was concerned that you might be feeling bad about what happened. I just wanted you to know I'm not angry or anything. The bouquet was a sweet idea."

I felt a lot better when I hung up. Mom and Dad were still talking in the living room. Mom was still worried about Robbie's habit of taking off his clothes. "You're a doctor," I heard her say to Dad. "If one of your patients had a child who was always undressing, what would you say?"

Dad looked thoughtful. "I guess I'd say the child doesn't like to wear clothes."

On Saturday Tim's swimming team had an extra practice in the afternoon, and Caroline was spending the day at a friend's house. I was wondering what to do when Jamie called and asked me to go to the roller-skating rink. I was a little surprised. At school all he wanted to do was hang around with Steve and Lester.

We had fun at first, skating around the rink as fast as we could. "This is fun," I said. "It's nice to be together without Steve and Lester."

"What's the matter with Steve and Lester?" Jamie bristled.

"Nothing," I said quickly. "I just don't like being with them all the time."

"I asked Steve to go with us," he said. "But he was camping with his Scout troop."

I saw that Jamie had a slightly guilty look. Then I understood. He had asked me only because Steve was busy. "I thought I was your best friend," I said.

"I asked you, didn't I?" Jamie snapped.

We skated awhile without talking. Finally, when we took a break, I tried to change the subject. "I'm trying to talk Mom and Dad into getting a dog."

"I don't like dogs. They always try to chase my cat," he said.

We didn't talk much after that. I thought about Miss Lawson while I skated around the rink. Miss Lawson was an animal lover. But she was the kind of person who would be happy for me, even if she didn't like dogs. That reminded me of my plan. I didn't think I'd better bring any more bouquets to school, but nothing could go wrong with a poem. Mrs. Sewall had promised that Miss Lawson would be back Monday morning. I decided to write a poem and put it on her desk when no one was looking. I knew she wouldn't tell anyone.

After dinner I got paper and a pencil and sat down at my desk. A poem shouldn't be too hard to write. I thought about some poems I'd heard:

Roses are red,
violets are blue.
Sugar is sweet,
and so are you.

That was too ordinary. Besides, Miss Lawson had probably already heard that one. I stared at the paper. Finally I wrote:

I love you, Miss Lawson.

Now I needed something that rhymed with Lawson.

I love you, Miss Lawson.
I think you're awesome.

Though that almost rhymed, it sounded dumb. I wished Mr. DeWitt had told me some of the poems he'd written to his wife. Caroline was good at writing, but I wasn't about to ask her. Tim had started locking himself in a closet every night, talking on the phone to a girl in his class named Alice. Still, I couldn't imagine him writing a poem. I even thought about asking Mom and Dad for help. But they would probably want to see what I was doing.

I tried again.

I love you, Miss Lawson: I think you're awfully pretty.
I hope you like me because I am so witty.
I think you are nice, and I think you are lively.
I'm sorry about your nose that you stuck in poison ivy.

I ripped up the paper and threw it away. Writing poems was not as easy as I'd thought.

12

Roses Are Red

MISS LAWSON WAS BACK Monday morning. Even with pink cream on her nose, she looked great. Just having her back at school put everyone in a good mood. She began to tell us about a new unit we'd be studying about life in medieval times. "A young man, often the younger son of a minor noble, entered the service of a knight. He was called a *page,* which meant he was little more than a servant. When he was fifteen or sixteen, he became a squire and his training really began."

While she talked, I found myself watching Willie. He seemed really interested. For once he listened without making a sound.

"What did the pages have to do?" Lisa asked.

"I imagine they had to serve the knight at dinner and polish the armor—things of that sort," Miss Lawson said.

"I bet they had to clean up horse poop." Willie jumped up and held his nose while he pretended to shovel. Everyone laughed except Miss Lawson.

"I'm sure they did, Willie," she said. Then she sighed. "Now, will you please sit down."

Before lunch we had gym. Mr. Laslo made Steve the captain of one of the kickball teams. Steve chose Lester first and then Jamie and me. Willie was the other captain. He ended up having to choose most of the girls. In spite of that, Willie's team won. Marcia played really well, but I didn't care because I was pretty happy with myself for making a couple of points for our team. Each time I made a point, Steve had pounded me on the back. "Way to go, Snodgrass," he said.

"That was a good game," I told Marcia when she walked near me.

She smiled a little shyly. "Well, thanks."

Willie's team started jumping around. "We won, we won," they bragged.

Lester pulled Jamie aside. "I know how we can get the girls *and* Willie," I heard him say. Then he stomped out of the gym.

It had been a fun game even though we'd lost, but now my good mood was ruined. As we walked back to our classroom to pick up our lunches, I wondered what Lester had planned.

Miss Lawson lined us up at the drinking fountain. While she was talking to another teacher, Lester and Steve slipped into the classroom. A minute later they were back in line, grinning and poking each other. I was the only one who had noticed they were gone.

"Where is my new sweater?" Amy wailed, a few seconds after we entered the room.

"My library book is missing, too," Marcia said. "I left it right here on my desk." Several other girls called out that they were missing things.

Miss Lawson looked upset. She made everyone look for the missing items. We searched under desks, in the cupboard, everywhere we could think of. The only one who didn't look was Willie. He was leaning back in his chair singing a song from a beer commercial, still happy after winning the game.

"Why aren't you helping us look?" I whispered.

"There are already twenty-two kids ransacking the room," Willie answered. He was right. The room had been completely checked. I saw that Miss Lawson was looking at him suspiciously.

After a minute Willie got up and walked to the pencil sharpener. The window beside the sharpener was slightly open, but he pushed it wider and stuck out his head. "There's all your stuff," he yelled.

Miss Lawson looked out the window. "What do you know about this, Willie?" she asked sharply.

Willie shrugged. "I just saw Amy's sweater down there on that bush."

Miss Lawson's eyes narrowed. She sent two of the girls outside to pick up everything. "I don't know who did this," she said, staring hard at Willie, "but it better not happen again."

Jamie was winking at Steve and grinning. It was a pretty funny joke on the girls. I just wished Miss Lawson hadn't blamed Willie. I tried to tell myself it was all right. After all, she hadn't punished him, and he was in trouble so often that once more probably didn't make any difference.

School settled into a busy routine. About a week later I arrived home just as Mom was going out the door. "I have to go to the ground-breaking ceremonies for the new hospital," she said.

"Are you going to give a speech?" I asked.

"A little one," she answered. "Then I'll dig up the first shovelful of dirt."

I stared at her. A mayor sure has to do some strange things.

The house was quiet. Robbie was still taking his nap, and Tim was at football practice. Caroline had stayed after school for a Writers' Club meeting. It was a perfect time to work on a poem. I wandered into the kitchen to get a snack. "Did anyone ever write you a poem?" I asked Mrs. Albright, trying to sound casual.

She was sitting at the table, folding a load of clean clothes. She shook the wrinkles out of a shirt and smiled. "Mr. Albright wrote me a little poem when he asked me to go with him."

"Do you remember it?"

"Let's see. I think it was something like: 'Roses are red, daisies are yellow. If you like me, then I'll be your fellow.' "

"That's kind of cute," I said. "Did you say you liked him?"

"How could I resist a poet?" Mrs. Albright said. "But that was the only poem he ever wrote."

"Did you ever write him a poem?"

Mrs. Albright looked a little sad. "I never did. I guess I'm not very good at writing things."

"I'll bet he liked your chocolate chip cookies and your chocolate cake, though," I said.

Mrs. Albright said, "That he did. Maybe he knew they were my way of saying 'I love you.' "

I wondered if Mrs. Albright ever got lonesome. A big family can be a pain, but maybe it would be worse to have no one at all.

I went to my room and stared at some blank paper. Then I scrunched it up and threw it in the wastebasket beside the desk.

After dinner I decided to ask Tim for help. He was heading for the closet with the phone.

"Are you going to call Alice?" I asked.

"Who?" Tim looked confused. "Oh, her. No, I'm calling Tiffany, so get lost."

I found Mom in the living room. "Do we have a book of poems?" I asked her.

She looked up from the papers she was working on with a pleased expression on her face. "I didn't know you were interested in poetry. Or is it for school?"

"It's for school," I said quickly.

Mom pulled a slim volume off the bookshelf and handed it to me. "I'm not sure if this will help. There are some nice poems in here, but they're mostly love poems."

I snatched it out of her hands. "That will be okay. Thanks." I dashed back to my room before she could ask any more questions.

I found a poem by Robert Burns on the second page. It was perfect. The only think wrong was that the poet must not have been a very good speller. He spelled *love* "luve," and he didn't know how to spell *melody*. I copied part of it carefully and fixed all the spelling.

O, my love is like a red, red rose,
That's newly sprung in June.
O, my love is like the melody
That's sweetly played in tune.

As fair art thou, my bonnie lass,
So deep in love am I;
And I will love thee still, my dear,
Till all the seas gang dry.

The last line sounded pretty weird, but since I didn't want to ask Mom what "gang" meant, I just left it.

13

The Great Snake and Poem Disasters

I HAD PLANNED to slip the poem on Miss Lawson's desk first thing in the morning, but when I walked into the room, everyone was crowded around Steve's desk. Curious, I dropped my books on my desk and squeezed in to see.

"It was in my backyard," Steve said.

A couple of the kids were making awful faces. "Gross," Amy shuddered. "I hate snakes."

Steve had brought a small aquarium. Inside was a small brownish garter snake.

"Do you suppose they had garter snakes in medieval times?" Charles asked.

"What if you were a knight and one crawled inside your suit of armor?" Willie joked.

"Oh, gross," Amy said again.

"It doesn't look very happy," Marcia said, her voice sympathetic. I was surprised that she wasn't one of the kids looking scared.

We're supposed to be in our seats when the bell rings, but Marcia was the only one who scurried back to hers just as Miss Lawson entered the room. Most of the kids stayed gathered around the aquarium. Miss Lawson didn't even notice. She walked over to Steve's desk and looked at the snake. She didn't seem nervous at all.

"Why does it keep sticking its tongue out?" Sara asked.

"I think the snake uses its tongue to sense where it is," Miss Lawson explained.

"You mean it can see my hand coming with its tongue?" Willie laughed. He reached in quickly and grabbed the snake out of the aquarium. In a flash the snake curled itself into a little knot. With a startled look Willie dropped the snake on the floor, and it quickly wriggled out of sight under the lockers.

Half the class stampeded toward the door, screaming at the top of their lungs. The other half, including Willie, stood paralyzed with shock. "Oops!" he finally said.

Suddenly the classroom door was thrown open, and Mr. Higgenbottom pushed his way through the crowd huddled by the door. "What is it?" he yelled. "Is somebody hurt? I heard the screaming all the way down in my office."

Miss Lawson pointed to Willie but couldn't seem to get out any words. She had come completely unglued. "There is a snake slithering around the room," she finally blurted out.

"Calm down, Miss Lawson," Mr. Higgenbottom said sternly. "We'll find it." He frowned at Willie. "I should have known you'd be involved in this."

Amy stood up on her chair to keep her feet off the floor. "I think I'm going to faint."

"In that case, sit down! Where is this snake?" Mr. Higgenbottom asked. Everyone stared at the empty spot where the snake had been only a minute before.

"Don't be such wimps." Marcia stood up and walked back to the lockers. "I think it went under here."

Willie bent down and looked under the lockers with Marcia. I hurried over to help, but a second later Willie reached into a dark corner with a triumphant yell. "Gotcha!"

Everyone by the door let out a collective sigh of relief.

Now that the snake was safely back in the cage, Miss Lawson looked embarrassed. "Maybe we should just let it loose outside," she suggested briskly.

"Excellent idea," said Mr. Higgenbottom. "I trust there will be no further commotion. Miss Lawson, may I have a word with you outside?"

Although I couldn't hear what Mr. Higgenbottom was

saying, I figured he was scolding Miss Lawson for letting the class get wild. When she came back in the room, her lips were pressed tightly together.

"Do you want me to take it out for you?" Willie offered, reaching for the cage.

"I certainly do not," Miss Lawson said grimly. "You have caused enough trouble for one day."

"I didn't mean to drop it," Willie said. "It surprised me when it wriggled like that."

"Martin can carry the aquarium outside and let it loose. Willie, sit down. And I don't want to hear another sound out of you for the rest of the day."

It seemed that Miss Lawson was angry mostly because Mr. Higgenbottom had scolded her. I picked up the aquarium. "I really think it was an accident," I said as I passed her desk.

"Willie has far too many 'accidents.' " Miss Lawson still sounded furious. "Like things falling accidentally out the windows, for instance."

For a second I was tempted to tell her that it wasn't Willie who had thrown the girls' things out the window. Then I saw the warning look on Jamie's face. If I told, all the boys in the class would think I was a tattletale. I wouldn't have to worry about being popular. I wouldn't have any friends at all. So I went outside.

I tipped the aquarium near the edge of the school's grassy front yard. A second later the snake whipped out of sight beneath some rocks.

When I returned to the room, Miss Lawson sounded more like herself. "Maybe we can read something about reptiles later," she said. "Right now I have a surprise for all of you."

Everyone sat up and listened. Willie was hunched over in his seat, daydreaming as he looked out the window. While I slipped into my seat, I knocked the paper with the poem off my desk. For a split second it hovered in the air, then slid along the floor by Marcia's desk.

"Hand it back," I hissed. For a second I thought she would. But she must not have heard me, because she unfolded the paper and, with a puzzled expression, started to read. My ears felt warm with embarrassment. Now she would probably blab it all over school that I'd written a love poem to Miss Lawson.

"As you know," Miss Lawson began, "we've been learning about medieval life. It was a time when serfs, or peasants, worked for wealthy landowners, who were called *lords*. Some of the peasants were free men and owned a little bit of land. Nevertheless, they had to spend part of their time working for the lord.

"These medieval lords often built great castles, which were more than just places for the rich to live. They served as centers of commerce and housed the lord's soldiers who protected the people in times of war.

"Marcia is preparing a report on castles, and I think you'll find they were not such a great place to live. But

85

last night I had a wonderful idea for this unit. I talked to Mr. Higgenbottom this morning, and he thinks it would be great, too."

While everyone was waiting expectantly, I was in agony watching Marcia finish reading the poem. Finally she did, and instead of handing it back, she folded it neatly and put it in her pocket. Without looking at me, she took out a piece of paper and wrote something. Then with a funny kind of smile, she dropped it on the floor and moved it toward me with her foot.

Miss Lawson was telling the class that we were going to turn the classroom into a castle. "Your parents can see it when they come to open house night," she said. "So let's make it really spectacular. The art teacher found us some big rolls of paper and cardboard we can use, and Mr. Higgenbottom says we can work in the cafeteria, where we will have more room." She passed around some books with pictures of castles and knights to give us ideas.

"Can I make some swords and fighting stuff?" Jason asked. He was usually very quiet, but he loved to draw war things. No matter what we were doing in class, Jason would be drawing tanks and planes.

As Miss Lawson was talking to Jason about swords and suits of armor, I reached down and picked up the note and read it.

Dear Martin,
I loved your poem. It is the first time anyone wrote me a poem. My mother explained that sometimes boys tease girls they like, so I understand why you were so mean the other day, and I forgive you. Do you want to be my boyfriend?
Love, Marcia

P.S. I think your red hair is nice.

I couldn't believe it. Marcia actually thought the poem was for her. She'd drawn some little hearts and flowers around the edge of the note. This was starting to be the worst year of my life. In the first two weeks of school, I'd managed to become best friends with a first-grader, cover my teacher with poison ivy, and now my worst enemy wanted to be my girlfriend.

14

Willie's Plan

I STARED AT THE NOTE trying to figure it out. Ever since first grade, Marcia had acted as if she hated me. Now she was beaming at me as if I were the greatest thing she'd ever seen. If I told her the poem wasn't for her, she would hate me for the rest of her life. That didn't sound like a bad idea, but looking at her, I knew something else. That poem had made her really happy. If I told her the truth, she would be really hurt. I gave her kind of a weak smile. Inwardly groaning, I glanced up at the clock. It was almost time for morning recess. Marcia was sure to corner me on the playground, and I needed time to figure out what I was going to do.

Miss Lawson motioned for me to come to her desk. "Would you mind giving up a few minutes of recess?" she asked. "I'm in need of a strong arm to help me carry some supplies to the cafeteria. Then, when recess is over, the class can get right to work."

My heart sang with happiness. Miss Lawson thought I looked strong. Out of everyone in the room, she had picked me. And she had given me an excuse to avoid Marcia.

I had barely sat down again in my seat when the bell rang. Jamie rushed over. "Come on," he said. "Steve and Lester want us to play football with them."

"I can't. I promised Miss Lawson I'd help her."

"She's not looking. Slip out and tell her you forgot," Jamie said.

Miss Lawson's back was to us. She was picking up a box by her desk. I shook my head. "She's counting on me to help."

Jamie glowered at me. Without a word he ran out to catch up with Steve and Lester. I hurried up to the desk and grabbed a big box. "If you would rather play outside, it's all right," Miss Lawson said with a smile.

"No, I'd rather help you," I said, gathering up a pile of cardboard. Maybe if Marcia had some time to think, she might remember that she hated me. That way the day wouldn't be a total washout.

By the time the bell rang to end recess, Miss Lawson and I were almost done. I grabbed the few rolls of paper that were left and joined the rest of the class lining up to go to the cafeteria. Marcia looked disappointed when she got Charles as a partner. I peeked at her over the paper rolls and saw her take out the poem and read it again. A little smile crossed her face before she put it back in her pocket. Obviously she hadn't come to her senses yet.

As soon as we got to the cafeteria, Miss Lawson divided us up into committees. Willie, Jamie, and I were the committee to transform the doorway to the classroom into a castle gate. Amy and Rachel looked disappointed. By now, everyone except Miss Lawson knew who had thrown their things out the window. And some of the girls acted as if they wanted Willie for a friend. Amy and Rachel hung around him on the playground and giggled every time he made a weird noise in class. I couldn't figure out why they liked him so much. Being Willie's girlfriend meant you had your hair pulled when you walked by or you got splattered from the drinking fountain every time Willie took a drink. If I were a girl, I wouldn't want to be Willie's friend.

"Why do Amy and Rachel like you so much?" I asked him, as we unrolled a big sheet of paper to cover the classroom door.

Willie looked thoughtful. "I guess it's because I don't give them bouquets of poison ivy." He laughed loudly, and Miss Lawson frowned. He leaned over and whispered, "Why? Do you want to ask one of them to be your girlfriend?"

"No," I whispered. "I'm trying to get rid of a girlfriend."

"Marcia Stevens," he said.

"How did you know that?" I sputtered.

"Marcia told Amy you wrote her a poem. You're really getting into this love stuff."

"It was a mistake. I don't want her for a girlfriend," I said. "I don't want a girlfriend, period."

Jamie had been sitting back on his heels, listening. Now he shook his head. "Just tell her you don't like her."

"I don't want to hurt her feelings," I said.

Jamie looked at me as if I were crazy.

"Hey, wait a minute," Willie said. "That's it! Pretend you really like her. Follow her around everywhere and write her mushy notes. Pretty soon she'll get sick of you."

"Do you think that will work?" I asked doubtfully.

"Sure," Willie said firmly. "You could even kiss her."

"I don't think I could stand that," I said.

"Or"—he paused for a moment—"you could give her one of your poison ivy bouquets." Willie and Jamie both laughed wildly.

"Willie," Miss Lawson said sharply. "If you can't work quietly, I will have to make you work by yourself."

"It wasn't his fault," I said. "I asked him something."

Willie flashed me a grateful glance. For the rest of the period we worked on our project and didn't talk. When we lined up to go back to the room, Marcia made sure she was next to me.

"You didn't answer my note," she said.

"I—I was thinking about it," I said. "What would I have to do if I was your boyfriend?"

Marcia shrugged. "I don't know. I never had a boyfriend. You could come over to my house, I guess."

When she saw me hesitate, Marcia added, "My dog just had puppies. You could see them if you came over."

"I'll think about it," I promised.

Marcia nodded as though she were satisfied. Then before we got back to class, she stopped. "You didn't write that note to be a mean joke or anything, did you?"

For a second I was too startled to answer. "W-what do you mean?" I stammered.

"Well, you wrote me that beautiful poem, and now you're acting kind of funny."

"I swear I didn't write it for a joke," I said. Although it was the perfect chance to admit that I'd written it for Miss Lawson, somehow I couldn't make myself say it.

She nodded. "You just must be shy. I thought so, but I had to make sure."

15

Tim's Surprise

I THOUGHT ABOUT visiting Marcia all the way home on the bus. I figured it wouldn't hurt to go to Marcia's house to see the puppies. And maybe Willie was right. Anytime now, Marcia was sure to remember she didn't like me.

Dad was sitting at the kitchen table eating a sandwich. "First chance I've had to eat lunch today," he explained. Just then Tim burst in the door. "Guess what?" he called out. "One of the eighth-grade varsity football players moved. They picked me to replace him."

Dad was putting on his jacket to go back to his office. "That's wonderful," he said, giving him a big bear hug.

I sighed. Dad likes sports, and I knew he was really proud of Tim. Sometimes I wished I was good at sports so he could feel that way about me.

"More trophies." Caroline sighed. "Someday the house is going to sink into the dust from the weight of all Tim's trophies."

"Jealous?" Tim sneered.

"Oh yes." Caroline sighed again dramatically. "I was absolutely longing to be able to run around being bashed to death over a stupid football. I'm simply devastated."

"It's more than being bashed," Tim said. "You have to memorize plays and study the other teams to find their weaknesses."

"Well, excuse me. I didn't realize that your trophies were a testament to your intelligence. Before I know it, you'll be in the gifted and talented program with me."

They were still at it when I went out and sat on the front steps. I took Robbie out with me and watched while he ran his little car around the steps. Mr. DeWitt saw me, shut off his hedge trimmer, and walked over.

"You look pretty glum," Mr. DeWitt said as he sat down beside me.

"Caroline and Tim are arguing about which one of them is the greatest," I said. "I was just thinking I'd like to be part of the argument sometime."

"I happen to think you are pretty great, too," he said.

"Thanks," I said. "But I wish there was something special about me."

"We all have something that makes us special. It's just that most of us don't get trophies to prove it. What's really important is how we feel about ourselves. You have to give yourself kind of an inside trophy." Mr. DeWitt patted my shoulder. "You've got lots of time to find out what your special thing is."

The door opened behind us, and Mrs. Albright stepped out. She looked embarrassed when she saw Mr. DeWitt. "Oh, I didn't know you were here, Mr. DeWitt. I was just checking on Robbie."

Mr. DeWitt whipped off the old cap he always wore. "Why, hello, Mrs. Albright. It's nice to see you again. But please, call me Harold."

Mrs. Albright looked more flustered than before. "All right, Harold. And then you must call me Agnes."

There was a minute of awkward silence that was broken when Tim ran out the door.

"Want to catch a few passes?" he asked me.

"No, thanks," I said. Actually, I agreed with Caroline's opinion of football. Getting mauled by ten-foot giants over a weird-shaped ball seemed like the worst kind of dumb.

"I'll catch a few with you," Mr. DeWitt said, as he put his cap back on. "I used to play a little football when I was in school."

I watched with amazement as Tim and Mr. DeWitt tossed the ball back and forth. Mr. DeWitt was pretty good for an old man. He was leaping after the ball and racing around the yard almost like a teenager. Tim could hardly keep up with him. I glanced at Mrs. Albright. I could tell she was impressed. "Boys will be boys," she muttered. Finally she shouted out, "Be careful, Harold. You're not as young as Tim, you know."

Mr. DeWitt caught a hard pass from Tim that nearly knocked him off his feet. "Don't you worry about me," he yelled, tossing the ball back to Tim.

"Ow!" Tim yelped. Just as he'd started to catch the ball, he twisted awkwardly and fell to the ground.

"Are you all right?" Mrs. Albright cried out, rushing over to his side. Mr. DeWitt stood with a stricken look on his face.

Tim groaned. "I think I twisted my ankle."

The three of us managed to get him up the steps and into the house. Robbie followed, patting Tim sympathetically.

Tim plopped down in a kitchen chair, and Mrs. Albright took off his shoe and sock. "It will probably be all right in a minute," he said. But his face was pale, and his foot was swelling. A faint purplish color was creeping up his leg.

At that point I heard Mom pulling into the driveway. "Go get your father," she said when she walked in the door and sized up the situation.

I ran around to Dad's office. It's in the back of the house and has its own entrance. As usual, the waiting room was full of people with appointments. Mrs. Baughman, the nurse, was surprised to see me.

"Hello, Martin. Is something wrong?"

I explained quickly, and she hurried away to tell Dad.

A grouchy-looking lady grumbled loudly as Dad came out of his office. "I was next," she exclaimed. "I've been waiting for forty-five minutes."

"I'll be right back, Mrs. Carson," Dad said soothingly. "I have an emergency to attend to. I'll be as quick as I can."

Tim winced when Dad felt his ankle. "What about football?" he whispered.

"It was all my fault," Mr. DeWitt said, still looking upset.

Tim bravely waved his hand. "It wasn't your fault at all. I landed wrong when I jumped. It's just twisted, right, Dad?"

"I'm afraid it might be broken. We'd better have an X ray taken, to be sure. I'll call ahead so they will be waiting for you. Then I'll meet you there as soon as I can."

Mom drove Tim and me to the hospital while Dad took care of the grouchy lady. Afterward Dad took me with him to look at the X rays. They were pretty interesting. I could see the shape of Tim's ankle bones, white against the black background.

"There's a tiny crack in the bone," Dad explained as he studied the pictures. "Do you see it?"

I could see the faint jagged line running across the bone.

"It must be kind of neat to be a doctor," I said. "Except when you have grouchy patients like that lady in your office."

"Mrs. Carson has reason to be grouchy. She has arthritis and is in a lot of pain. It's very difficult for her to get around."

"I didn't know," I said, suddenly feeling horrible. "Can you help her?"

For a second Dad looked sad. "A doctor can't cure everybody. I'm trying to make her more comfortable."

"Tim's ankle can be fixed, can't it?" I asked, looking back at the X ray.

Dad nodded. "In a couple of months it will be as good as new. But I'm afraid football is out, at least for this year."

Tim took the news well, although he was pretty glum. I sat in the emergency waiting room while a cast was put on his foot and he practiced a bit with a pair of crutches.

The hospital smelled good. I'd been here a few other times with Dad, but this time I really paid attention. I watched the nurses bustling around and listened as doctors were called on the intercom. A man with a cut finger came in. He was holding a blood-stained handkerchief around it. A mother carried a baby who was crying because of a stomachache. A girl I'd seen at school showed me the big bump on her head that she got falling down her basement stairs.

Mom came out to check on me. "Are you getting bored waiting out here?" she asked. "I could have Mrs. Albright drive over and get you."

I shook my head. "This is a great place," I told her. "I've been thinking that maybe I'd want to be a doctor like Dad when I grow up."

"I bet you'd be a good one," Mom said. "You are a very caring person." To my embarrassment, she bent over and kissed the top of my head.

At last Tim was allowed to go home. A huge cast covered his foot except for his toes. "I can't go to school like this," he protested. "Everyone will laugh."

Caroline looked at him and shook her head. "The girls will love it."

Tim cheered up immediately. "Do you really think so?"

Caroline nodded. "Just tell them you were wounded playing football." She paused. "I'd leave out some of the details, though, if I were you. You probably won't want to mention that you were injured catching a ball thrown by a sixty-five-year-old man. As a matter of fact, I might be able to forget that, too. For a price, of course."

16

Zits, Fleas, and Other Terrible Problems

TIM STAYED HOME from school the next three days. Mrs. Albright took care of him during the week, but on Saturday he decided I would be his personal slave. He managed to kill any sympathy I felt for him in about two hours. He spent his time with his foot propped up on a footstool, barking out orders like a three-star general. Caroline was smart enough to suddenly remember a science report that required her to spend most of the weekend at her friend Mandy's house. I saw her stuff two teen magazines in her folder, so I figured the only things they were going to study were clothes and makeup.

I was the one who ended up fetching glasses of juice, snacks, books, pencils, and anything else Tim could think of to keep himself amused. Even worse than that was the remote control for the television. Tim insisted that he needed it close by because he had to hobble across the room with crutches. But putting a remote control in his hands was dangerous. He couldn't resist changing the station every five minutes.

By Sunday, after watching ten programs in a half hour, I needed to plan an escape. Also, Marcia had called, and she was bugging me about when I was coming to her house.

"May I go to a friend's house Monday afternoon?" I asked after dinner. "It's pretty close to the school," I added. "I can walk there if someone could pick me up."

"Of course," Dad said, looking up from a medical journal. "Do you mean Jamie?"

"No," I said. "It's another friend."

"What's his name?" Mom asked, putting down the drawings of the new highway.

"Marcia," I mumbled.

Mom and Dad exchanged surprised looks.

"She has some new puppies she wants me to see. If I stay home, Tim will just think I'm his personal servant again."

Dad nodded. "I think Tim needs to go back to school."

"Do you think he's ready?" Mom asked. "There are a lot of stairs at the junior high."

They were so involved in the discussion about Tim that they forgot about me. I escaped before they could ask any more questions about Marcia. I was feeling pretty smug. I could get away from Tim, see the puppies, and make Marcia happy. And if I was lucky, no one would even know.

"I can pick you up after my meeting," Mom said at breakfast the next morning. "Doesn't Marcia live right next to Jamie?"

"Marcia?" You could almost see Caroline's ears prick up. "You're going to Marcia Stevens's house?"

"I'm just going to look at her puppies," I growled.

"I can't believe it. Martin has a sweetie pie." Caroline smirked. "Martin and Marcia sitting in a tree, k-i-s-s-i-n-g."

"That's enough," Mom said.

Tim was looking at me strangely. "I suppose you have something to say, too?" I asked.

"Not me," Tim said. "I think it's great. My little brother, the ladies' man. I didn't start liking girls until this year. Would you like to borrow my mousse?"

"Moose?"

"It's stuff to put in your hair," Tim explained.

"What's wrong with my hair?" I asked, patting my hair nervously.

"Nothing," Tim said. "But mousse makes it stay down smoother. The girls like it. I use it on mine all the time."

"Makes you look like a grease pit," Caroline said.

"If Caroline hates it, it must be great stuff," I agreed.

Dad took a last sip of coffee. "I'd better get to my patients. It's either that or we will have to take out a loan to pay for all this hairspray and mousse."

"And zit medicine," Tim added ruefully.

Robbie liked that word. "Zit, zit," he chortled, banging on the table with his spoon.

Caroline's hand flew up to her chin, covering a tiny red spot, but not before Tim had noticed.

"Aha. I'm not the only one who needs it."

"I do not," Caroline sniffed.

"Do too."

Caroline flounced out of the room, ending the argument.

"Want me to show you how to use the mousse?" Tim asked through a mouthful of toast.

I shook my head. "I don't really want Marcia to like me any more than she already does. I'm just going to see her puppies."

Mom announced that she was ready to drive Tim to school. She had decided to do this so he wouldn't have to get on the bus with crutches.

Caroline ignored me as we walked down the driveway. "I don't know why you're mad at me," I said. "I didn't say anything about your zit."

"It's not a zit," Caroline hissed. "It's a mosquito bite."

I peered a little closer. "No," I said, trying to be helpful. "I think it is a zit. But it hardly shows," I added hastily when she suddenly burst into tears.

"I'm ugly," Caroline sobbed. "Go ahead—admit it. All the other girls in my room have a figure. And most of them are taller. I'm just short and ugly."

"You're not ugly," I said.

"If you weren't my brother, would you think I was cute?"

"I guess so," I admitted reluctantly as the bus pulled up to the house.

Looking a little happier, Caroline climbed on board. Her red-rimmed eyes didn't escape Freddie, though. As usual, I sat down next to him.

"What's the matter with your sister?" he asked.

"I think she's worried because she has a zit," I whispered.

Freddie twisted around in his seat and stared at Caroline, sitting in back with her friends. "What are you looking at?" she growled at him.

"I wanted to see your zit," he said in a loud voice.

I grabbed his arm and pulled him down in the seat. "You don't say things like that," I told him.

Freddie shrugged. "She asked me what I was looking at." He leaned over and whispered in my ear, "Girls are weird, aren't they?"

I nodded in agreement.

"My girlfriend likes to kiss me," Freddie said. "She chases me every recess."

"Why don't you tell the teacher to make her stop?" I suggested.

Freddie looked at me as if I were crazy. "I like it," he said.

Freddie's remark made me think. What would I do if Marcia kissed me? In school I watched her out of the corner of my eyes. She certainly didn't look like the kissing kind. Just to be on the safe side, I decided I'd better not stand too close to her.

After class started, Miss Lawson passed back the math test we'd taken on Friday. She had given us some problems figuring out how many stones we'd need to build a castle. "Jamie and Martin got every one right," she said as she handed them back. She'd stamped a happy face on mine. "Everyone did a good job. Almost everyone," she added as she handed Willie his paper. Everyone in class could see the big red *D* on the top. He made a face as if he thought it was funny, but he turned bright red.

After math we worked some more on the castle walls. Everyone was getting excited about open house. In addition to making the castle, each group had to do a report about the Middle Ages. Amy and Sara were doing a report on the foods people ate. Miss Lawson was going to help them prepare a medieval feast. Our group was doing a report on knights. I was surprised that Willie had found some interesting facts for our report. "The knights were given land," he said. "But in return they had to fight in the king's army if he needed them." Actually we were having a good time working together, except that Jamie was unhappy he was not with Steve and Lester.

Jason had made some cutout knights to stand guard and some cardboard swords and shields. Each knight also had a war hammer and a mace for smashing armor. Jason pretended to have a sword fight with Steve. Miss Lawson laughed.

Then Willie grabbed a sword. "I wish I'd lived then and been a brave knight. I bet it was fun to fight dragons," he said.

Miss Lawson frowned. "Put the swords away before they get bent."

Willie flashed the sword in a giant *Z* before he put it down.

"The book I'm reading for my report says that castles weren't so great," Marcia said. "They were damp and cold. And the people were dirty and had fleas," she added.

"You are right," Miss Lawson said. "People had not learned very much about cleanliness. Still, it was a great time in history. Martin, do you know why?"

I froze. How could she do that to me? I hadn't even

raised my hand. I tried to think. "Uh . . . Maybe because people were starting to think about building great things, and making laws, and dreaming about being heroes," I said.

Miss Lawson beamed at me. "That's a wonderful answer. You are very perceptive."

I wasn't sure exactly what perceptive meant, but from the way Marcia was beaming at me and Willie was scowling, I thought it must be something pretty good. I tried to imagine Miss Lawson as a medieval damsel in distress. I thought about her leaning over the castle wall, calling for help. I charged up on a mighty war-horse. "I will save you from the dragon," I shouted. My armor clanked as I leapt down and drew my sword. The dragon was fierce, with fire roaring from his wicked mouth. Boldly I confronted him. Then I noticed that the princess was scratching herself. She picked something off her arm and flicked it down. "Fleas," she explained.

"Fleas!" I jumped out of my chair. Everyone laughed, and I realized I'd said it out loud. Miss Lawson was giving me a strange look. She probably didn't think I was so perceptive after all.

"Sorry," I mumbled, sitting down.

After school I put on my coat very slowly and pretended I was looking for something in my desk. I hoped most of the kids would be gone so they wouldn't see me walking with Marcia. Jamie played the trumpet, and I knew his lesson was right after school on Mondays. Probably he wouldn't see me, either. Marcia waited by the door, but after a minute she came back inside. "What's taking you so long?" she asked.

"I, uh, forgot my math paper," I said, stuffing it into my book bag. Slowly I followed her outside. I scanned the playground quickly and gave a sigh of relief. Almost everyone had gone. The buses were just pulling away from the curb, and the walkers were almost out of sight. Then I noticed Willie and a couple of the fifth-grade boys playing on the monkey bars. We would have to walk right by them.

"Why don't we walk this way?" I asked, pointing in the other direction.

"Because my house is this way." Marcia put her hands on her hips and stared at me. "You sure are acting weird."

"I just wanted to walk around the block with you," I said, thinking quickly.

Marcia shook her head. "My mom will get upset if I don't get home in a couple of minutes. Come on."

Marcia walked rapidly down the street. With a sinking feeling I followed, pulling my coat collar up around my face. With a little luck Willie wouldn't even notice me.

I didn't have a little luck, though. Just as we reached the end of the playground, I heard Willie shout, "Hey, Snodgrass. Where are you going with your little honey-bunch?"

17

Puppies, Plays, and a Little Romance

I CRINGED with embarrassment, but Marcia giggled and called back, "Martin's just coming to see my new puppies."

Willie jumped down from the monkey bars and ran over. "Can I see them, too?"

Marcia hesitated. "My mother is expecting only one person for company."

"I'll look at them and then leave," Willie promised. "I really like animals, especially dogs."

"I guess that would be all right." Marcia nodded.

Willie fell into step beside us. He didn't know that he was really helping me. Since both of us were going to her house, no one would tease me about being Marcia's boyfriend.

"I thought Miss Lawson was kind of mean to you today, Willie," Marcia said conversationally. I stared at her, surprised and annoyed. Miss Lawson mean? She had been a little grouchy, but she would never be mean.

Willie shrugged. "Teachers never like me."

"Maybe they would if you would do your work and not make all those noises in class," Marcia said primly.

"I don't want to shock them by being too good." Willie grinned, but his eyes were clouded. "Besides, my grandma says I'll probably end up no-good like my dad."

"Your grandma must be mean," Marcia said.

"No, most of the time she's nice. She only says that sometimes when she's mad at me," Willie said.

"It's still a terrible thing to say," I exclaimed. "My dad says you can be anything you want to be if you work hard enough."

Willie gave me a hard look. "That's an easy thing to say when your dad is a doctor and your mother is the mayor. Everyone in your family is a big shot. Everyone in my family is a nobody."

"My dad is pretty important," I admitted. "But I'm not really like him. So why do you have to be like your dad? Besides, my friend Mr. DeWitt says everyone is special in some way."

Willie just shrugged. He seemed to be thinking about something.

"Isn't our room great?" Marcia asked, obviously trying to change the subject. "Miss Lawson makes school so interesting. I'm learning a lot about medieval times."

We talked about our projects until we arrived at Marcia's house. Mrs. Stevens looked surprised to see Willie. She was an adult version of Marcia, with the same round glasses and her hair pulled back with a barrette. Behind her I could see into the living room. It was spotlessly clean. Even the magazines on the coffee table were perfectly lined up. She stood blocking the door, as though trying to decide if it were safe to let us in.

"Why don't you take the boys around to see the puppies," she finally told Marcia. "When you're finished, come in the back door. Be sure to wipe your feet."

Marcia was embarrassed. "My mom's kind of fussy about the house," she explained as she led us out to a shed in the backyard. A small black-and-white dog with a freckled-looking nose whined and wagged her tail when we opened the door. She sniffed at Willie and me and allowed us to pet her.

"This is Mitzi. Better let her get used to you," Marcia warned. "Then she won't get upset when you touch the pups."

I saw a little black-and-white head peek over the side of the basket in the corner of the shed. Suddenly the basket tipped over, and we were covered with wiggling, licking balls of fur. Willie and I sat on the shed floor and allowed ourselves to be attacked. Marcia hovered over us, looking like a proud mother.

"Do you think your mom and dad would let you have one?" Marcia asked.

I'd already picked out my favorite. He was almost all white, with one black ear and a spot on his back and paws that were three sizes too big. While the others nipped and pulled at our clothes and tumbled over one another, he had snuggled comfortably in my lap.

"I know Mom and Dad would give in if they saw the puppies," I said.

"I wish I could have one." Willie's voice was filled with such longing that it made me sad. "But my grandma would never agree."

"If I get one, you can come over and play with it," I promised impulsively. Willie's answering smile made me feel good.

Mitzi climbed back in her basket. One by one the puppies forgot us and curled up next to their mother. We sat beside the basket, still watching and talking. I told them about my friendship with Mr. DeWitt and growing a garden last summer.

"That sounds like fun," Willie said. "I saw your name in the paper when you won a blue ribbon at the fair."

"The only trouble is that the pumpkins got ripe so early," I said. "Now it's almost Halloween and we'll have to buy one to carve."

"I wish my mother would let me have a garden,"
Marcia said. "She doesn't like me to get dirty. She
worries about germs and bugs."

"Some bugs are good," I said. "Mr. DeWitt says lady-
bugs and praying mantises are good because they eat
harmful bugs. And worms break up the soil."

"I used to save worms," Willie said. "After it rained,
I'd pick them up off the sidewalk."

I laughed. "Me too." It was strange. The three of us
were having fun just talking as if we were old friends. I
couldn't talk like that with Steve and Lester, or even
Jamie anymore. Steve and Lester were mostly interested
in sports and in talking about how great they were.

Mrs. Stevens looked in the shed door. "Come in the
house and wash your hands, and you may have a
snack." She paused and gave me a curious look. "Have
you ever been in a play?"

"No," I said, "except in the first grade. I was a tree,"
I added.

"This year the Youth Theater is putting on a play
based on *The Adventures of Tom Sawyer*. With your red
hair you'd be perfect for the part of Tom," she said.
"Why don't you try out?"

"What would I have to do to try out?" I asked.

"Everyone who signs up will be in the play. If you
want a lead part, you should read the book and then act
out the part you like. Have you read the story?"

I shook my head. "I saw a movie once, but I don't remember much of it."

"Tom lives with his aunt Polly. He's always getting into mischief, especially with his friend Huckleberry Finn. It was written a long time ago by Mark Twain." She paused. "The play we are doing is a musical, so you'll want to prepare a song."

"Sing?" I croaked. But Mrs. Stevens didn't hear.

"Can anyone try out?" Willie asked.

"Oh, certainly," Mrs. Stevens answered. "There will be a lot of parts to cast."

"I've been in the last three plays," Marcia said. "It's really fun. Wouldn't it be great if we all did it together?"

Mrs. Stevens gave Willie a doubtful look before she nodded. "That would be nice."

While we were talking, Mom parked in Marcia's driveway and we all walked over to meet her. She got out and introduced herself to Mrs. Stevens.

"Oh, Mayor," Mrs. Stevens gushed. "I was just telling your son that he would be perfect in our Youth Theater production of *Tom Sawyer*. Of course, being in a play is a big commitment. He would have to be very responsible about coming to rehearsals."

"Martin is a very responsible boy," Mom said. To me she said, "Would you like to try out?"

I nodded eagerly, but my mind was whirling. Mom

117

had said I was very responsible. Maybe she would think I was responsible enough to have the puppy.

"Before we go, you've got to see their puppies," I pleaded. Reluctantly Mom allowed Marcia and me to lead her back to the shed.

"Oh my." Mom laughed when the puppies tumbled onto her. My puppy came right to me. "This is the one I like best," I said. "He likes me."

"They're not quite ready to leave their mother," Marcia said. "But you could have him in a week or two."

"I'll talk to Dad," Mom said finally. "Maybe it's time we made a decision."

"I'll take care of him all by myself," I said. "And think how happy a puppy will make Robbie."

"We'll discuss it," Mom repeated firmly. Then she smiled in a way that made me hopeful.

"Are you sure you would like to be in a play?" Mom asked as we drove home.

"As long as I don't have to be a tree," I answered, remembering my first-grade play. The tree costume was made of paper, and it made me itch. I was supposed to wave my branches in the wind. But I waved too hard and knocked over another tree beside me. Everyone had laughed when we both fell on the floor.

"Mrs. Stevens said I looked just right to be Tom Sawyer. That's the lead part."

"You'll have to work really hard if you want the part," Mom said. "Just having red hair isn't enough."

"Mrs. Stevens said I should read the book," I said.

"Don't wait too long to pick out a scene to learn. The tryouts are in three weeks."

I closed my eyes and imagined myself on the stage, with hundreds of cheering people clapping as I took a bow.

"I was thinking about being a doctor when I grow up," I said. "Maybe I'll be a famous actor instead."

Mom smiled. "Let's see if you get a part before you make plans to move to Hollywood."

18

Green Eyelids
and a Warning

WE STOPPED at the library and checked out a copy of *The Adventures of Tom Sawyer* before we went home.

Of course Caroline had a few things to say. Things like, "Oh, barf. Who'd go to a play with Martin in it?" She picked up the book and thumbed through it.

"Probably everyone in town," I said smugly.

"Good things don't come automatically," Dad said. "Usually you have to work for them."

"This looks like kind of fun," Caroline said. "Maybe I should try out, too."

"Oh, now you're talking about something really

gross," I said, throwing up my arms. "I'm going to talk to Mr. DeWitt. He can give me some advice. I wonder if this is how his son started acting."

Mom washed her hands as she started cooking dinner. "He's not home. Mr. DeWitt is taking Mrs. Albright out to dinner."

"You mean like a date?" I asked.

Mom nodded. "Isn't that sweet?"

"Sweet?" Caroline exploded. "I think it's ridiculous. Mr. DeWitt has white hair, for heaven's sake."

"I never heard of a law saying that people with white hair couldn't date," Dad said.

"I think it's silly," Caroline said. "Dating's for teenagers."

I laughed. Caroline reads teen magazines that tell girls how to fix their hair and how to get boyfriends. So even though she has never even had a boy call her on the phone, she thinks she's an expert on dating. When I remind her that she is not even a teenager, she gets mad and says she wants to be ready.

I remembered the silly way Mr. DeWitt had acted the day Tim broke his ankle, and how Mrs. Albright had been so flustered. "Mr. DeWitt may just be tired of eating dinner by himself. I think it's nice that they're going out together."

"You are so utterly, utterly *dumb*," Caroline said.

"Of course, I wouldn't be lonesome with a cat like

121

Daffy for company," I said, looking at Mom. "Or even better, a dog."

At bedtime I asked Mom if she had talked to Dad about the puppy.

"We'll talk about it tonight," she promised. "By the way, have you started the book?"

I'd forgotten all about the play. "I forgot, but I'll do it tomorrow," I said. "I still have plenty of time."

The next morning Mrs. Albright was up bright and early and seemed unusually cheerful. She hummed softly as she stirred the oatmeal and made buttered toast for breakfast.

Tim and Caroline exchanged knowing glances. "Did you have a nice dinner last night?" Caroline asked.

"It was lovely," Mrs. Albright said. "Mr. DeWitt is a wonderful dancer."

"You went dancing, too?" Caroline looked stunned. "Do you think that you'll go out again?"

"I think we might," Mrs. Albright answered. She dished up a bowl of oatmeal for Robbie and set it in front of him.

"Yuck," Robbie said. He pushed his bowl away, slopping the milk out on the tray of his high chair.

"None of that, young man," Dad said firmly. "You eat it. It's good for you."

Robbie shook his head. "Yucky stuff bad. Robbie wants a cookie."

"If you take a bite, I might tell you about a surprise," Dad said.

Robbie scowled, but he took a tiny bite. I sat up straighter. A surprise could mean only one thing.

"Your mom and I talked it over last night. Martin's friend has some nice puppies, and we've decided to take one. That means everyone will have to pitch in and help."

"Too bad my ankle is broken," Tim said. "I won't be able to help much."

"I saw you last night," Dad said. "If you are well enough to balance yourself with that cast and shoot baskets, you are well enough to help with a little puppy."

"Puppy," Robbie echoed happily.

"Can it sleep with me?" Caroline demanded.

"It was supposed to be my dog," I said. "And Robbie's," I added, remembering the argument I'd used with Mom.

"Any pet will have to belong to the whole family," Mom said, pouring herself a cup of coffee. "We are certainly not going to get four pets. If there is going to be arguing over it, we may change our minds."

No one complained after that. I had an interesting thought. If I stayed friends with Marcia, I could go to her house and visit the puppy. By the time we brought him home, I was sure he would like me the best. I smiled at

Caroline. "Maybe we can teach him tricks together," I said innocently.

Caroline squinted her eyes suspiciously, but she nodded. I stared at her. Something looked different. "Your eyelids are green," I exclaimed.

Dad put down his morning paper. "What is that on your eyes?" he asked.

"Mold." Tim laughed so hard at his own joke that he sprayed little drops of milk.

Caroline gave us both killing looks. "It's just a little eye shadow. All the girls wear it. You wouldn't even have noticed if it hadn't been for blabbermouth."

I hadn't really meant to tattle. It had simply taken me by surprise. I could see Caroline wasn't going to believe that, though.

"Wash it off, honey," Mom said. "You're not old enough to wear makeup."

"All the other girls wear it," Caroline protested.

"All the other girls are older than you," Mom pointed out. "And I think sixth grade is too young for them, too."

Caroline turned to me. "You just ruined my whole year in sixth grade, you little tattletale."

"I didn't tattle," I said. "But it does make you look even dumber than usual."

I expected Caroline to say something awful back, as she usually did. Instead she began to cry and ran upstairs. Mom gave me one of those I'm-disappointed-in-you looks and followed her.

"What is wrong with her?" I asked, truly bewildered. "She is really acting strange lately."

Dad sighed. "Sometimes growing up is a little rocky. You boys could help by being a little nicer to her."

"I don't think I want to grow up," I said.

"Can't be helped," Dad said cheerfully. "It happens to all of us."

"At least I'm not dumb enough to get all excited about not having green eyelids," Tim said, cramming another piece of toast into his mouth.

"How excited would you get if we took away your mousse?" Dad asked.

"That's different. I need that to look good," Tim said. "Nothing Caroline does will make her look good. Unless she painted on a whole new face," he added with a cackle.

By the time the bus came, Caroline was ready, although her eyes looked a little red instead of green. "I really am sorry," I said. She sniffed and turned her back to me. She still hadn't spoken to me when we boarded the bus. She headed back to sit with her friends.

I twisted around to check. She didn't seem to be the social outcast she had predicted. As a matter of fact all her friends were crowded around her sympathetically.

Freddie had been absent a couple of days, and I was

almost glad to see him. Life sure is simple when you're in the first grade. He told me how he'd gotten sick at school all over his desk and the custodian had cleaned it up. He had eaten spaghetti for lunch, and he described in great detail what it looked like. "I don't want to be a custodian when I grow up," he announced cheerfully.

Jamie met me at the front door. "Why do you hang around with that little first-grader?" he asked, right in front of Freddie. "And my mom saw you at Marcia's house with *Willie*. People are going to talk about you."

Some of the kids standing nearby snickered, and I felt my face getting hot. "I have to sit with Freddie on the bus because there is nowhere else to sit. And I'm not really friends with Marcia and Willie. I just went to Marcia's to look at her puppies," I answered loudly. "Willie tagged along."

Freddie gave me a hurt look before he hurried to his classroom.

I told Jamie what Mrs. Stevens had said about the play, but all the time I was thinking about what I'd said.

"None of the cool kids care about Youth Theater," Jamie said. "It sounds kind of dumb."

"I think it sounds like fun," I said. I was getting pretty tired of Jamie. All he thought about anymore was being popular.

"What if you forget your lines?"

"I don't have any trouble memorizing things. Wasn't

I the first one in class to learn the times tables last year?" I reminded him.

Steve and Lester walked up behind us. "My dad got a new pinball machine for our game room," Lester said. "Do you want to come over tomorrow and play?"

"That sounds great," Jamie said eagerly.

"It does sound like fun," I agreed, just as the bell rang.

After class started, Miss Lawson read us a book about St. George fighting this terrible dragon. I noticed that Willie was sitting still and listening. The room was starting to look like a castle, I thought as I looked around. The reading loft was covered with brown paper with a stone design, so that it was like a tower. Even the cupboard where the paper supplies were kept had been transformed into an armor room. Willie, Jamie, and I were almost finished with the door. We'd made an arch, and now we were making banners to hang for decoration. Our parents were going to be amazed on open house night.

"Do you want to come over tomorrow and visit the puppies?" Marcia asked as we went out for recess. "Willie's going to come, too. We could help each other learn something for the play."

"I can't. I'm going to Lester's tomorrow," I said. Actually I thought that playing with the puppies sounded better. But I knew Jamie would never understand.

"Don't forget what I told you," Jamie whispered, after

Marcia had run off to join a group of girls jumping rope. "If you want to be popular, you can't hang around with a bunch of nerds."

"I'm not," I snapped. We spent recess listening to Lester brag about his new pinball machine. I didn't hear much because I was thinking about Marcia. Last year I thought she was just a pain in the neck. But for a girl, she wasn't so bad. And now that I knew Willie a little better, I knew he was really nice. I was the one who was awful, pretending that they weren't my friends.

19

I Never Saw
a Purple Cow

WE WENT to either Lester's or Steve's house almost every afternoon for the next couple of weeks. Lester had about a hundred video games and a whole room full of pinball machines. When we went to Steve's house, we played in his indoor pool. I was the only one who didn't know how to swim. I splashed around in the shallow end while the others had races, but it was still fun.

Now that Jamie and I were friends with Steve and Lester, it seemed as if everyone wanted to be with us. I was invited to two birthday parties, and at recess kids who had hardly talked to me before asked me to join their games. I should have been happy, but I wasn't. I did have fun with Steve and Lester, and it was nice having so many friends. Still, sometimes I saw Willie looking at me, and I remembered the good time we had at Marcia's house.

I finally was able to go to Marcia's house on Saturday afternoon. To my surprise, Willie was already there.

"You're not mad because Willie's here, are you?" Marcia asked, while Willie was chasing one of the puppies that had gotten loose. "I mean, you're my boyfriend, but you're so busy with Steve and Lester that you hardly talk to me. And Willie wanted me to help him practice for the play."

"Why would I be mad?" I asked. "I like Willie."

"Really? You hardly talk to him, either," Marcia said accusingly, just as Willie came back.

"My grandma has been helping me practice for the auditions," Willie said. "She's all excited about my trying out for the play. She told me *Tom Sawyer* was one of her favorite books when she was young."

"What scene are you doing?" Marcia asked.

"I haven't decided," I admitted.

"You'd better hurry up," Willie said. "The tryouts are next Saturday."

I planned on beginning *Tom Sawyer* as soon as I got home, but Steve called and invited me to spend the night at his house. So I put it off once again.

* * *

"Do you need any help preparing for the audition?" Mom asked on Thursday night.

"No, I'm doing all right," I answered. Actually, I had barely started reading the book.

"I'm going to try out to be Aunt Polly," Caroline said. "If you're Tom, I get to chase you around with a switch and rap your knuckles."

"Why do you do that?" I asked.

Caroline put her hands on her hips. "Land sakes, child. I do believe you don't even know the story," she said with a southern accent. "I've half a mind to take a switch to you."

"You'd better keep your half a mind, since that's all you've got," I answered.

"That's a half more than you have," Caroline sneered. "At least I had brain enough to give myself more than two days to prepare for the audition."

Two days! Suddenly it hit me. Where had the weeks gone? I hurried to my room, determined to make up for lost time. Then I calmed down. It would be all right. I could finish the book tonight and decide on a part to learn. Tomorrow I would practice. I could hear Caroline singing "Camptown Races" in the kitchen. I closed my door so I didn't have to listen, and picked up the book.

Saturday afternoon came much too soon. "Martin, hurry or we'll be late for the tryouts," Mom called for the third time. Reluctantly I closed the book and grabbed my coat.

We piled into the car, and a few minutes later Mom parked in front of the building where the tryouts were being held. Inside the door, I stared in amazement. There were at least twenty kids, all looking as scared as me, and more were arriving every moment. Marcia was there, looking starched and nervous.

"I didn't know there would be so many kids," I gasped.

Mrs. Stevens went to the front of the room and explained about the play. "Now you may not get the part you try out for," she said. "We are going to make videotapes, and then we will look at them during the next few days and decide where you will do the best. I want all of you to make a real commitment. Every part, even the tiniest one, is important in a play."

A woman gave each of us a number. My number was twenty-four, and Caroline got twenty-three. I settled down to wait. Caroline pulled a copy of *Tom Sawyer* out of her pocket. I could see her lips moving as she practiced her lines again. I wished I'd thought to bring one. Now there was nothing to do except get more nervous with every passing minute.

I spotted Willie coming in the door. He was wearing a clean shirt, and his hair was neatly combed.

"I never asked you what part you wanted," I said.

"Tom Sawyer," he said. He waved his arm up and down, pretending to paint. "This is a great way to spend an afternoon," he said. "I'll bet there isn't one boy in a thousand, maybe two thousand, who could do this job just right. You just go on to the old swimming hole. I'm enjoying painting this old fence."

Several people had gathered around. When Willie finished, they clapped.

Willie looked up and grinned. "That's not exactly the way the book says it . . ."

"That's the part I want," I interrupted.

Willie looked at me. "Anyone can try out for it." He sat down beside me. "That was very good," Mom said, leaning over to smile at him.

I slouched in my seat. My own mother was acting as if Willie was so great. Even Caroline had clapped. I was too scared to talk much.

Willie was nervously humming "The Blue-Tail Fly." "That's the song I'm singing," he said when I looked at him. "I don't want to forget the tune. I'm so scared my stomach hurts," Willie added.

I was surprised he would admit he was scared. "Mine, too," I said. "It feels that way when I have to read in front of the class."

"If you goof around in class, the teachers think you're dumb and they don't call on you," Willie said quietly, so that Mom couldn't hear.

Suddenly what Willie had said hit me. "A song. I forgot about learning a song."

Mom sighed. "Martin, I offered to help you several times. Just sing something you know."

One by one, numbers were called, and nervous-looking kids went into a smaller room where the auditions were being held. I thought frantically of the songs I knew. "The Star-Spangled Banner" was the only one I knew all the words to.

Caroline went first. When she came out, she looked pleased. "They said I had a wonderful speaking voice," she announced.

"Did you get a part?" I asked.

"They'll post the cast list on the door next Saturday," Caroline said.

Before I could ask any more questions, Mom gave me a little push toward the door. "They've called your number twice. Hurry before you lose your turn."

My hands got clammy and my mouth went dry. Numbly I walked to the little room and shut the door behind me, wishing I could fall through the floor.

"Don't be nervous," someone said. There were three women and a man sitting at a little table. Mrs. Stevens smiled at me encouragingly. A video camera was on a tripod near them.

The man asked me my name and grade and jotted them down as I told him. "Now then," he said briskly. "What are you going to do for us?"

"In the beginning of the story, Tom has a fight with a new boy," I said slowly.

"Go ahead," said Mrs. Stevens.

I opened my mouth, but nothing came out. What was it that Tom had said? I stood there in panic, trying to remember. Why hadn't I practiced longer? I'd been so sure of myself, and now they were probably thinking I was a real dummy.

"Perhaps you could recite a poem," Mrs. Stevens suggested.

I thought of the poem I'd copied for Miss Lawson. My mind had gone completely blank. All I could do was stare at the video camera and try not to get sick. Finally, in desperation, I blurted out the first thing that came into my mind.

> *"I never saw a purple cow;*
> *I never hope to see one.*
> *But I can tell you anyhow,*
> *I'd rather see than be one."*

There was a moment of silence. Mrs. Stevens had that look grown-ups get when they think you're not doing your best, but because you're a kid, they don't want to hurt your feelings. Finally the man chuckled and handed me a script. He pointed to some lines. "Try reading these lines," he said. "Use a lot of expression."

By now I was starting to feel dizzy as well as sick to my stomach. I couldn't seem to focus my eyes on the script. Then I realized they were the same lines Willie had done for us while we were waiting. I tried to remember how he had acted. He'd made it sound as if he were having a great time painting the fence. I read the lines, but I kept thinking about the story Freddie had told me on the bus a few weeks ago. I wondered if there was a custodian in this building. My stomach was churning dangerously. What if I got sick and they made me clean it up? I imagined myself cleaning while they all stared at me with these really disgusted looks.

"That was fine," Mrs. Stevens said. "We also need you to sing a little bit for us. Did you prepare a song?" The man got up and went to the piano.

" 'The Star-Spangled Banner,' " I croaked. At least I remembered the words to that. I croaked through a few bars. My voice got sort of squeaky on the high notes.

"Well, that didn't take long," Mom said when I stumbled out of the door. I stared at her. It seemed as if I'd been in there for hours.

Willie was next. "Good luck," I said as we got ready to leave.

"Thanks," he said grimly. I saw that he was as nervous as I had been.

Caroline chatted cheerfully all the way home. "I just know I'm going to get a good part. They really seemed to like me. How about you, Martin?"

"Me too," I said, trying to sound confident. Mrs. Stevens had said that everyone would get some kind of part in the play. But why did I have this feeling that I was going to be the only kid in the whole history of the Youth Theater who was asked to stay home?

20

Do Beetles Have Feelings?

LUCKILY FOR ME, I had the puppy to keep my mind off the play. I went to Marcia's on Sunday to visit him again. The puppy really acted as if he knew me. As soon as I walked in the door, he came over, crawled in my lap, and licked me with his little pink tongue. I named him Sam because it seemed to suit him.

"I'm glad you are taking him," Marcia said. "I want all the puppies to have a good home, and I can see that you really love him."

After we played with the puppies, Marcia asked me to go into the house and play some games. I wasn't very comfortable around Mrs. Stevens, but it was a little too cold to stay outside. Mom wasn't picking me up for another hour.

Mrs. Stevens gave us a snack and acted pretty friendly. At least she didn't mention how awful I'd been at the audition. After we ate, we went to Marcia's room. I was amazed to see an electric train set that took up about half of the room.

"Hey, this is great," I said. The track wove in and out of tunnels and hills, and there were roads, signs, and a little cluster of buildings that made a town for the tiny people.

Marcia seemed pleased. "Do you like it? It's my hobby. Every Christmas and birthday I ask for something new for it."

"I had a train set. Not as neat as this one, but it was fun. My little brother broke it," I said glumly.

"Bring it over. Maybe I can fix it," Marcia said.

"You can fix electric trains?"

"Sure. It's not too hard if you know how they're made and you have the right tools. My dad teaches me a lot about fixing things."

"My dad's not very good at fixing things," I said. "Except for people," I added.

"Why don't you pick a game we can play?" Marcia suggested, pointing to the cupboard full of brightly colored boxes. Most of the games at our house had pieces missing because Robbie had gotten into them. Marcia's looked almost brand-new.

"It must be nice to have brothers and sisters to play with you," she said. "I hardly get a chance to play with any of my games. I guess that's why I like the trains so much. I can do that by myself."

"I think it would be nice to be the only kid in the family." I laughed. "Maybe we should trade." Marcia had gone to school with me since kindergarten, yet I was beginning to realize I hadn't known her at all.

"I know that poem wasn't for me," Marcia said suddenly.

I almost bit my tongue in shock. "It's all right," she said. "I knew it all the time. I was just hoping you'd be friends with me. But I never figured out who it was really for."

"Miss Lawson," I mumbled.

Marcia stared at me. For a minute I thought she was going to laugh, and I knew I wouldn't like her quite as much if she did. But she only said, "She is awfully pretty."

"She's beautiful," I exclaimed.

"I wish she was nicer to Willie."

I nodded. "Me too. Maybe she would be if he'd quit making all those noises in class and acting dumb."

"I think he acts up in class to make himself special. Dumb, but special."

Mom came to pick me up before we could talk about it anymore. "I'll come over again in a couple of days if I can," I said as I left.

"Are you coming to see Sam?" Marcia asked as I was zipping my coat.

"Yes," I answered honestly. "And to see you, too. I had a really good time."

"You don't have to be my boyfriend," Marcia said. "I mean, you are a boy and all, but maybe we could be just friends."

"Sure," I said, feeling good about everything. I could be friends with Marcia after school, and no one would have to know.

Jamie was waiting for me when I got off the bus the next morning. "I saw you leaving Marcia's house yesterday. You're going to spoil everything. How come you're always playing with girls and babies?" he asked loudly.

"How come you're worried about it?" I snapped. I turned away and walked inside the school. I slammed down my books on my desk and slumped in my seat. Why did life have to be so complicated? I wished I was Robbie's age again. All he had to worry about was how to get his clothes off without Mrs. Albright catching him. For a minute I almost understood Caroline. She worried about zits and having her hair just perfect, and about being the only girl in the room who didn't have a boyfriend. Maybe growing up just meant you had more and more to worry about.

I sat in my seat without even looking at Marcia or Willie.

Miss Lawson tapped her desk. "We are going to work on long division today, class."

Willie raised his hand. "Can I sharpen my pencil? It broke."

Miss Lawson looked suspicious, but she nodded. Willie strolled casually by me. As he passed, a note fell on my desk. I covered it quickly with my hand. I waited until Miss Lawson turned to write on the blackboard before I unfolded the note.

Would you like to come to my house Saturday? My grandma said it would be okay.

I looked at the note for a long time before I turned around. I guess it was too long. Willie's lips were pressed together and then he mouthed, "Forget it."

For the rest of the morning Willie acted up in class. During silent reading he hummed and whistled. And when we had a social studies quiz, he got out of his seat and walked all around the room. After Miss Lawson said he had to stay in the room for lunch, he looked almost pleased. I kept thinking about what Marcia had said as I watched him.

Jamie seemed to have forgotten our argument by lunch. Steve and Lester were huddled in a corner with several other boys from class, and Jamie motioned me over. They were all acting really interested in something on the ground. Once in a while they would laugh. I pressed in to see what they were doing.

"Lester found this huge beetle," Jamie explained. I peered over his shoulder at the beetle. It was flipped over on its back, frantically twisting its legs to right itself. Every time the beetle would start to flip right side up, someone would push it over again. Everyone thought that was pretty funny. As the beetle wiggled and squirmed, they all laughed. A kid named Jon from the other fourth-grade class was poking the beetle with a rock, cracking its shell with a crunchy noise, but not killing it.

"You don't have to torture it," I exclaimed.

"We're just playing," Jamie said. "Don't be such a baby."

The beetle was ugly. I wondered if beetles felt pain.

"If we cut off some of its legs, it won't be able to move and we can play with it after school," Lester said. "I wonder how long it'll live with no legs."

I stuck out my foot and stepped on the beetle hard enough to kill it.

"Hey!" Lester said. "Why did you do that? We could have played with it later."

"I don't like to see things suffer," I said. I could hear angry murmurs as I walked away.

"What a nerd," Lester yelled to no one in particular.

"You better go play with your girlfriend," Jamie called after me.

Sam was waiting for me when I got home from school. Mrs. Stevens had delivered him earlier in the afternoon. Mrs. Albright had already covered the floor of the back porch with thick papers and put an old rug in a box for a bed. Robbie was sitting in the doorway, watching the puppy's every move with shining eyes. "My doggie," he informed me.

Sam wagged his tail so hard that his whole body wiggled. I picked him up and buried my nose in his fur. Mrs. Stevens must have given him a bath, because he smelled soft and sweet. I got a burning feeling in my throat, and my nose started to run. This had been one of the worst days of my life, but with one lick of a tiny pink tongue, everything seemed better. For a little while I didn't have to think about Willie or Marcia, or even how dumb I'd been to try to protect a stupid beetle that probably didn't even feel pain.

21

Puddles and Plays

No puppy in the history of the world had more attention than Sam that night. Mom and Dad laid down a strict rule. Sam had to stay on the enclosed back porch or outside until he was housebroken. Everyone except Robbie took turns all evening taking him out. He loved it outside. He ran around the backyard, chasing every fallen leaf that moved and sniffing every blade of grass. As soon as we brought him back to the porch, he went on the papers. When Caroline found out we were required to change the papers, she promptly lost interest. She announced that she had tons of homework and disappeared into her room. Tim changed the papers once, holding his nose and muttering, "Gross." Then he, too, disappeared.

I couldn't believe that one puppy could go so many times in one night and still miss going outside. Dad had bought a book on puppy care. It said to praise a puppy when he did it in the right spot, and pretty soon he would get the idea. But how were we going to praise him if he never even accidentally went outside?

By Friday I was getting worried.

"Do you suppose he's not very smart?" I asked Mrs. Albright as she wiped off the counters after dinner.

"You know how Robbie still wets his pants? Well, the puppy is even younger. It may take several months to train Sam," she said cheerfully. "Sooner or later he'll slip and go outside."

Mr. DeWitt knocked on the door. "I had to see this wonderful pup I've been hearing about," he said, kneeling and giving Sam a pat. Sam promptly rolled over so Mr. DeWitt could scratch his stomach. "We'll have to introduce you to your neighbor Daffy," Mr. DeWitt told Sam.

Then he stood up and twisted his cap in his hands. "I was wondering if you would like to go to a movie," he asked Mrs. Albright.

Mrs. Albright looked pleased. "If you can give me a couple of minutes to get ready, I'd love to." They stood there for a minute smiling at each other. It made me feel good to watch them.

Mr. DeWitt left to get his car. Mrs. Albright hurried to finish her work.

"Do you think you and Mr. DeWitt will get married?" I asked suddenly.

Mrs. Albright seemed startled. "My goodness, child. Whatever made you ask that?"

"I was just thinking," I mumbled.

Mrs. Albright sat down beside me at the table. "I like Harold. A lot. But it takes time for love to grow. First you get to be really good friends. I guess Harold and I are in that stage right now. We're finding out all the things we both like, and the ways we are different." She patted my arm. "No matter what we decide, I'll still be here. You are like my own family."

Caroline came down from doing her homework to get a snack as Mrs. Albright walked out the door. She poured herself a glass of milk and sat next to me. "They're sure getting lovey-dovey."

"I think it's kind of nice," I said.

"You would. You're such a dweeb," Caroline said automatically. I thought maybe she was getting used to the idea. She took a big drink of milk. "Are you excited about tomorrow?"

"What's tomorrow?"

"You *are* a dweeb. The play. Tomorrow is Saturday. We find out if we got a part."

I had forgotten, but I nodded. "I knew that," I said, trying to sound nonchalant.

"If I don't get a good part, I'm going to drop out," Caroline said.

"Mrs. Stevens said every part was important."

Caroline snorted. "I have my reputation to think about. It's bad enough being the only girl in sixth grade who doesn't wear makeup," she said pointedly.

"Your friends still like you," I reminded her.

"All the most popular girls wear makeup," Caroline insisted stubbornly.

"Why not be happy with the friends you have," I said. I started choking on the words before they were halfway out of my mouth. Wasn't I doing the same thing? The truth was, Jamie and I had grown apart and I didn't even want to be friends with Lester and Steve. But I did like Willie and Marcia and even little Freddie. What was better, they liked me.

Saturdays are usually great days. It had rained during the night, however, a drizzly, foggy rain that left a gray gloom over the morning. It didn't help to find that Sam had made several messes on the porch floor, missing the papers completely. Naturally Tim and Caroline slept in, so I was the one who had to clean up. I was washing my hands when I saw Willie ride up on his bike.

"Hey, come on in," I said, opening the back porch door.

"I was just riding around," Willie said shyly. He noticed Sam sitting in his box. "You got him," he exclaimed.

"I think we have to change his name to Puddles, though." I explained our difficulty in getting Sam to go outside.

"Why don't you give him a big drink of milk?" Willie suggested. "Then take him outside and make him stay there until he goes. Sooner or later he's got to slip up. I could stay and help you watch him."

We went to the kitchen to get some milk. Dad had come down for breakfast and heard Willie's idea. "That sounds like a great idea," he said, pouring coffee into his cup. "I don't think it will be that easy, but it might be a start. Why don't you have some breakfast with us first?"

Willie shook his head. "I better not," he said reluctantly.

"Don't be silly. I'm going to make pancakes," Mom said, walking into the kitchen and heading for the coffeepot like Dad. "And I make great pancakes."

While we ate, the sun peeked through the gray curtain of fog. We gave Sam milk until his little tummy bulged, and headed outside with him. Mom put on Robbie's jacket so he could tag along, with a warning for us to keep an eye on him, too.

Willie bent over, picked a stranded worm off a large rock, and threw it into the damp grass where it could wiggle away. When he saw me watching, he looked sheepish.

I grinned at him. Willie galloped around the yard, playing horse with Robbie. Willie was wild and noisy, and Robbie loved it. I tried to imagine Lester playing so patiently with a little kid like that. One of Lester's favorite games was called bumper cars. He and Steve ran through the little kids playing hopscotch, bumping into them so hard that they almost fell over.

After Mom took Robbie inside, Willie and I sat down on the ground. It was still damp, but we leaned against the trunk of the tree and watched Sam sniffing a line of industrious ants that were carrying breakfast home to their nest.

"My grandma taught me the song I sang at the try-outs," Willie said. "When I auditioned, one of the ladies said I should think about being a singer. Wouldn't it be weird if I became a famous singer or actor someday?" In the middle of talking, he jumped up and yelled, "He's doing it!" and pointed at Sam.

Sure enough, Sam was doing his business right beside some bushes. We pounded each other on the back with glee, making so much noise that poor Sam cowered behind a bush.

"Good puppy," I said, patting him on the head.

Wiggling with pleasure, Sam bounded beside us as we ran in to tell Mom and Dad the news.

"He did it," I exclaimed. "Sam went outside. Now can we let him in the house?"

Mom looked past me at Sam. "I'm afraid you have a bit more work to do," she said, pointing to the new puddle beside him.

Sam was sent back to the yard in disgrace. By noon he had gone twice more outside and once more in the house. "He's getting better," Willie joked, as he got ready to leave. "That's three to two."

Dad came outside as Willie pedaled off down the street. "I like your new friend," he remarked. He bent over and gave Sam an encouraging pat as he spoke.

"You do?" I must have sounded surprised, because Dad's eyebrows shot up. "It's only that Miss Lawson doesn't like him very much. I guess I thought most grown-ups would be like her."

"Maybe Miss Lawson hasn't looked hard enough," Dad said mildly.

"I think that, too," I said, voicing the thought that had been troubling me. "I mean, she's a really great teacher. I mean, she's so beautiful and all. And she has great ideas. I'm learning a lot of neat stuff about history and all sorts of things."

Dad sat on the porch beside me. "Don't be too hard on her. No one is perfect, you know. This is Miss Lawson's first year teaching. She's still learning, too."

That was an interesting idea. I'd never thought about

adults learning. I guess when you're a kid, you just figure they know everything.

Dad clapped his hand on my shoulder. "I'm heading to the hospital to look at some test results. Since you like hospitals so much, perhaps you might like to come with me. After that we can check the cast list for the play and see if you are going to be a famous movie star."

"What kind of tests are you checking?" I asked as we climbed in the car.

Dad looked serious. "I have a patient who has been very sick. At first I thought it was the flu, but she kept getting sicker. So I asked her a lot more questions, and finally she remembered that she had gone on a picnic the day before her symptoms started."

"A picnic made her sick?" I asked. I sat up a little straighter. Dad was discussing his case with me as if I were an adult.

"It was last weekend, when it was so warm," Dad explained. "The lunch was in the cooler, but it sat in the hot sun all day while she and her friends went for a hike."

"Food poisoning!" I said.

Dad grinned at me. "That's what I'm hoping. I know how to treat that. My patient recalled that the deviled eggs tasted kind of warm."

"Being a doctor is like being a detective, isn't it?" I said as we pulled into the parking lot.

Dad nodded. "Sometimes," he said.

We went straight to the hospital lab, and Dad introduced me to the technicians. "This might be Dr. Snodgrass the second," Dad joked. He put his arm around my shoulder. "That is, if Hollywood doesn't get him first." The technicians laughed. One of them showed me around while Dad studied the reports. He even let me look at some blood in a powerful microscope.

Dad looked pleased when he finished the reports. I knew without his saying anything that he had been right. I felt almost as happy as if I'd been the one to figure the case out. It was great to think about your own dad really helping people and saving lives.

When we finally arrived at the Youth Theater, there was a small crowd gathered by the door. I made my way to the front and scanned the list for my name. It was clear down at the bottom. "Boy tricked into whitewashing fence" was written beside it. My heart sank. That character had only about two lines to say.

"Willie got the part of Tom Sawyer," Dad said.

"What?" I screeched. But sure enough, Willie's name was at the top of the list.

Dad chuckled. "Caroline is Becky Thatcher. That means she'll be Willie's girlfriend."

"Marcia is Aunt Polly. Everyone got a good part except me."

155

I stomped back to the car. "It's not fair," I stormed. "Willie got the part I wanted."

"Maybe next time you will prepare better," Dad said quietly.

I knew he was right but I was still unhappy. "Willie wouldn't have even known about the part if he hadn't barged in when I was with Marcia."

Dad gave me a disappointed look but didn't comment. I pressed my lips together and hunched in the corner of the seat. When we arrived home, I clumped up to my room and slammed the door as hard as I could. I could hear Dad downstairs talking to Mom and Caroline. I flopped on my bed and stared at the ceiling.

"Oh no," Caroline said, loud enough for me to hear. "I have to pretend a fourth-grader is my boyfriend."

Tim stuck his head in the door. "That's tough, about not getting your part," he said.

I shrugged. "It was a stupid part anyway."

Mom came in next. She sat on the edge of the bed and glanced around the room. "When I was in school I wanted to be a cheerleader. I practiced and practiced. I was so sure I was going to make the squad. Then my best friend, Mary Beth, got picked instead of me."

I sat up and looked at her. "Were you mad?"

Mom nodded. "I was so jealous I wouldn't speak to Mary Beth. I told myself that she was acting stuck up because she was a cheerleader. But she was just the same. I'm the one who ruined our friendship. Although we made up later, it was never the same."

"I didn't practice very hard," I admitted.

Mom nodded. "I think Willie did. Maybe he practiced harder because he needs this part more than you do. This may be the very thing that will help him gain some self-confidence."

"I guess I'm really mad at myself for not practicing," I admitted as I lay back down on the bed. "Willie deserves the part. He even practiced with Marcia."

Mom nodded. "Willie's not going to change overnight. Still, I think this play could be the start of something very good for him."

22

A Medieval Open House

THE WEEK OF our open house, we didn't get much work done in school. Monday, everyone was busy either putting the last-minute touches on our classroom decorations or brushing up on our facts. When the parents came, each committee had to stand by its project ready to answer questions. A couple of the mothers had made tunics for all the boys. That's a kind of shirt they wore in medieval times. Most of the girls had managed to find long dresses or skirts, so we all looked our parts.

"Would you help me carry all the leftover supplies to the art room?" Miss Lawson asked just before lunch on Tuesday.

I was glad that she asked me. It gave me a chance to talk to her about Willie. As we walked down the hall with our arms filled with papers, I took a deep breath. "I've wanted to tell you something for a long time," I said.

Miss Lawson smiled. "What is it, Martin?"

"Do you remember the day someone threw all that stuff out the window?" I began. "It wasn't Willie. And there've been other times that you thought he did something that he didn't."

We reached the art room. Miss Lawson replaced the rolls of paper in the supply cabinet before she answered.

"I wish you had told me this sooner," she finally said. "Who was it?" Then she shook her head. "Never mind, I think I know."

"Willie is kind of noisy and he doesn't like to sit still," I said quickly. "But he really is nice."

Miss Lawson nodded. "And you think I'm too rough on him?"

"Sometimes," I said uncomfortably.

"I have been thinking about that myself," Miss Lawson answered gravely. "Although you are right when you say Willie is too noisy, I have never seen him do one mean thing to anyone. And since we've been working on this project, he's really doing much better in class," she added thoughtfully.

"I hope you're not mad at me for saying something," I said.

159

"Of course I'm not angry," Miss Lawson said. "As a matter of fact, I wish you had talked to me sooner. This is my first year teaching, and I need all the help I can get."

"I think you're a great teacher," I said.

Miss Lawson grinned and gave me a little hug. "Thanks. I think you are a great student."

I felt really good walking back to the classroom. Miss Lawson had talked to me as if I was an adult.

A lot of kids from the other rooms were finding excuses to walk by and peek at our room. Most of the other rooms had projects on display too, but nothing like ours. Mr. Higgenbottom toured the "castle" and smiled at Miss Lawson. "Well done," he said. "I'm going to see if the paper will send a photographer this evening."

Just before school ended Miss Lawson called Willie and me up to her desk.

"Could both of you come a little early tonight?" she asked.

Willie looked worried. I suppose he thought he was in trouble. But Miss Lawson gave him a reassuring smile. "The Youth Theater had two knight costumes in their wardrobe," she explained. "They let me borrow them. Since you two are going to be greeting everyone who comes in, I thought you should wear them."

"What about Jamie?" I asked, trying to be fair. "He worked on the project with us."

160

"Jamie's going to be the lord of the castle," Miss Lawson said. "He will escort people around to see everything."

That night nearly every parent came to open house. Mr. Higgenbottom said later that it was the best open house the school had ever held. All down the hall near our room were market stalls, and some of the kids pretended to be merchants. Willie and I stood by the door with our swords crossed. When anyone came Willie shouted, "Lower the bridge!" It was really a large piece of cardboard held up against the door by ropes. That had been Willie's idea, and everyone agreed it was terrific.

Inside the classroom Jamie led parents around to see the sights. Amy and Lisa were in one corner weaving on a loom borrowed from Lisa's mother. Kyle guarded the arms closet and answered questions about medieval weapons. Steve and Lester pretended to cook a feast and had to answer questions about food. They kept giving Willie and me jealous looks all night. Marcia sang a ballad. That's a song that tells a story. Ballads were one of the ways medieval people found out about the news.

Freddie and his mom came by, with my family right behind them. Freddie got all excited when he saw us in our knight costumes. "I wish I was in fourth grade, too," he said.

"So do I," Caroline said. "We never got to do anything like this."

The photographer came and took a lot of pictures for the newspaper. And Mr. Higgenbottom walked around beaming at everyone, even Willie. Willie's grandmother was there, too. As we left, I heard her telling Mr. Higgenbottom about Willie getting the lead part in *Tom Sawyer*.

Suddenly I started to laugh.

"What's so funny?" Dad asked.

"I was just thinking about how this play is supposed to be so good for Willie. But he might not feel that way."

"Why not?" Mom asked.

"I'd like to see his face when he realizes that in the second act he has to kiss Caroline."